多雷插图本

THE RAVEN 乌鸦

爱伦·坡 诗选

[美] 埃德加·爱伦·坡——著

刘象愚 董滨——译

吉林出版集团股份有限公司

目录

CONTENT

译序

知道爱伦·坡（Edgar Allan Poe, 1809—1849）文名的人大概不少，许多人都知道他是美国文学史上著名的小说家，可能读过他的《厄舍古屋的倒塌》《莫格街凶杀案》《金甲虫》等名篇，然而知道他还是文学批评名家和大诗人的读者恐怕就不会太多了。事实上，坡不仅以《厄舍古屋的倒塌》《莱吉亚》《泄密的心》等怪诞、恐怖意味极浓的短篇厕身哥特式小说名家的行列；以《莫格街凶杀案》《被窃的信》等作开创推理、侦探小说的先河；以《气球骗局》《汉斯·普伐尔历险记》《瓶中手稿》《瓦尔德马病例真相》等作与儒勒·凡尔纳、威尔斯一起成为科幻小说的"发明者"；而且以《创作的哲学》《诗的原理》等文章成为著名批评家队伍中的一员，在这些文章中他提出"美"是文学创作最高境界、短篇小说以立"效果"为先、作家必须高度关注艺术效果的有机统一性和整体性等观点，从而为短篇小说做出了重要的理论贡献；更值得指出的是，坡还是大诗人，为世界诗歌

史增添了《乌鸦》《艾尔·阿拉夫》《帖木儿》《乌拉路姆》《安娜贝
儿·李》《莱诺儿》等经典诗篇。

坡一生发表的诗作一般认为只有60余首，数量虽然不多，但佳作却不
少。他的诗歌大都是任性率真之作，往往以饱满的情感，直抒胸臆，
既不故作深沉，也不忸怩作态，无论长歌，还是短章，无论写人，还
是写事，读者都能从这些吟唱中直接不隔地感受到诗人的喜怒哀乐，
看到和听到一个真诚、善良的灵魂在娓娓诉说。坡的诗充满了瑰丽的
想象和奇特的意象，极富象征色彩；同时又极富音乐美，他在传统诗
歌格律的基础上腾挪变化，巧用善用尾韵、头韵、内韵、叠句、副歌
等手段，以或多或少的诗节，或长或短的诗句，造成或舒缓流畅，或
跌宕起伏，或抑扬顿挫，或迂回曲折的声韵效果。

坡少年时代就展示了非凡的诗歌天赋，在早期创作中就写出了像《帖
木儿》《湖——致》《十四行诗——致科学》《致海伦》《艾尔·阿拉
夫》《海中的城市》《以斯拉斐尔》《不安的山谷》等脍炙人口的篇
什。《帖木儿》和《艾尔·阿拉夫》两首较长的诗以奇幻绚丽的想象闻
名。在前者中，诗人让弥留之际的帖木儿向神父忏悔，表达个人野心
与纯洁美好的情感之间的冲突；在后者中，诗人从《可兰经》第7章借
来阿拉伯观念中表示天堂与地狱中间地带的名字"艾尔·阿拉夫"做
诗的题目，力图说明人无法获得永生，只有追求崇高的美，才能避开
人间的恶。《以斯拉斐尔》同样从《可兰经》借取灵感，诗人以东方

天使以斯拉斐尔自许，表达歌颂真善美，鞭挞假恶丑的意志。这首诗以浓郁的东方色彩和奇特的想象，获得了与英国诗人柯勒律治的《忽必烈汗》同样崇高的地位。《十四行诗——致科学》表达科学抹杀艺术、美和创造力的思想；《致海伦》表达了诗人在情窦初开的年华对美好爱情的憧憬。

坡晚年的诗作以《乌鸦》和几首悼亡诗最著名。《乌鸦》是象征性极强的作品，采用诗人常用的"年轻美人之死"的题材，通过一位老学者和一只突然飞进屋内的乌鸦的夜话，表达对已故恋人的深切怀念。在一个凄风苦雨的子夜，主人公独坐窗前，深陷在怀念已逝的恋人的感伤中，由于过度悲伤，他的精神处于恍惚状态，这时一只硕大的乌鸦不期而至。他向乌鸦问话，而乌鸦的回答始终是"不再"（nevermore）。乌鸦原是不祥之鸟，它象征黑暗、痛苦、悲伤、死亡，诗人通过这一高度象征性的意象，表达一种美人已逝，艺术灵感也即将枯竭的极度悲哀。全诗108行，通押[o:]的长韵，并用大量的头韵、内韵，编织成一首极富声韵之美的作品，成为英语诗歌中不朽的经典。《乌拉路姆》和《安娜贝儿·李》写于诗人妻子弗吉尼娅死后，是著名的悼亡之作。诗人哀叹爱妻的离世，在表面平静的文字下，抒发了一种极其真挚而痛苦的怀恋之情。

坡生前和身后一段时间在美国文坛的声誉颇具争议，然而他的名声却在欧洲大陆，特别是法、德、英诸国获得了高度认可。法国象征主义诗人波德莱尔、马拉美、瓦雷里高度推崇他，波德莱尔把他引为自己的"同类"、"兄弟"；马拉美写诗赞扬他是"凯旋的天使"；瓦雷里说他是创造世界的上帝，是"从空虚中创造形式"的"唯一没有缺憾的作家"；纪德把他看作"内心独白"的创造者之一。在德国，尼采、里尔克、卡夫卡等巨擘都对他大加赞赏；在英伦三岛，狄更斯、丁尼生、斯温伯恩、叶芝、萧伯纳、哈代等也充分肯定他的创作才能。经过百年的曲折历程，坡最终在自己的故国确立了牢固的文名。今天，坡已经毫无疑问地成为19世纪美国文学的经典作家，被公认为现代主义的鼻祖之一。

大约20年前，我曾为《外国文学名家精选书系》编选过《爱伦·坡精选集》，也编选过坡的短篇小说集。《精选集》中选收了《乌鸦》《安娜贝儿·李》《海中的城市》等12首诗。五六年前，徐家康先生意欲出版多雷插图本爱伦·坡诗集，希望由我承担翻译的工作，我因为已有《乌鸦》等旧译，便欣然接受了他的邀约。

多雷是19世纪法国著名艺术家，以版画和文学作品插图知名。他曾为《圣经》《暴风雨》《堂吉诃德》《失乐园》《神曲》《古舟子咏》《巨人传》《乌鸦》以及巴尔扎克和拜伦等人的作品做过插图。记得当年读王维克先生译的《神曲》，书中就附了多雷的插图。现在摆在读者面前的这个本子，就是采用多雷插图的一个选本。

这个选本选收了坡的二十九首诗，是其全部诗作的近半数。除《艾尔·阿拉夫》《乌拉路姆》等较长篇什外，其余名篇大都收入了，它包括了诗人不同时期不同类型的作品，有像《乌鸦》《帖木儿》等叙事色彩较浓的长篇，也有抒情色彩鲜明的短作，应该说，它大体上能够反映坡诗的基本面貌。

本书由我的夫人董滨女士与我一道完成。除《乌鸦》等几首长诗由我独立翻译外，其余短章都是她首先译出初稿，然后由我润色修改后定稿的。董女士出身于一个诗书之家，她的祖父早年入山西大学堂西斋读书，因成绩优异被保送留美，进匹茨堡大学学冶金，毕业后不久获冶金工程师称号，旋即谢绝美企业的邀请，毅然回国，参与山西兵工与冶金等领域的开创与奠基工作，为国家做出过重大贡献；她的父亲是资深文史学者，一生在师范学校教授文史地等课程。她喜读文学作品，能写一笔娟秀的小楷。大学因与我同学而结识、成婚。我们夫妻结发近50年，她为支持我在学业上的追求，牺牲了自己的爱好，把对我的爱与深情默默地融入料理家务、教育后代以及为我誊写书稿、校改文字等琐碎的劳作中。每当想到她为我做出的牺牲与奉献，我的歉疚之情便油然而生。摆在读者诸君面前的这本书是我们的爱情除两个女儿外的第三个结晶，也是我们恩爱一生的纪念。我要大声地说：我对她的爱与感激将随我终老。

需要说明的是，坡的一些诗作从手稿到随后在期刊杂志发表，其题目或文本不少都有过修改，而由此产生的不确定性完全可能导致同一首诗出现不同题目的两种或数种文本。这个选本作为一个双语对照本，其原文均采自当今被学界认可的版本。译注中所指该诗的首发时间同样也可能存在某种不确定性。

此外，还须对本书的翻译说几句。大家知道，诗歌是一种可诵读的文学形式，它有声韵方面的限制，显然，这种独特的形式特征对诗歌的翻译提出了更高的要求，一方面它要求译文既忠实于原诗的意义，另一方面又要紧随原诗的韵律，可是，要做到这一点却是相当不容易的，也许正是在这个意义上，诗歌的翻译成了文学翻译中最难把握的一种。

前文在一些具体分析的文字中曾说到坡对诗歌音乐性的刻意追求，为此，他在诗歌创作中尝试了不同的格律和韵式，对诗行、诗节、句式做了各种安排，采用了包括标点符号在内的辅助手段，因而极大地增强了诗歌的音乐性，造成了跌宕起伏，回环往复的美感享受。聆听有关坡诗的诵读，我们当不难体认到这一点。然而，另一方面，对诗歌音乐性的过分关注则又很可能使诗句的意义变得不那么显豁，譬如，有时为了押韵不得不颠倒正常词序；为了格律的需求不得不改变句式；有时为了强调顿挫而过多使用破折号等，这些现象在坡几首著名的长诗中都时有显现。一方面是音乐性的极大增强，另一方面是诗意清晰度的减弱，这种情形显然对翻译形成了更大的挑战，从这一角度似乎可以说，译诗难，译坡诗更难。

我们在三年前就完成了译事，当时交出的译稿已经经过了数次修改。这次修改原以为短期内可以完成，可是开始修订后却发现并非如此。我们对照原文多次仔细修订，在反复校改过程中不断聆听坡诗的各种诵读，这种聆听对我们助益甚大，它使我们在对坡诗的音乐性获得更深感触的同时，也使我们认识到，我们的译诗同样应该具有较大的可诵读性，否则，即便在诗意和诗韵上百分之百地忠实，也不能算满意的坡诗翻译。抱着这样的理念，我们在修改过程中不再坚持亦步亦趋地追随原诗韵律的初衷，而是参酌汉诗的韵律加以折衷变通，以便在整体上保持译诗在诵读中的音乐性。我们时而完全抛开原诗，反复诵读译诗，时而又仔细对照原诗，检查译诗在意义与韵律等形式方面的忠实度，以期在尽量突出译诗音乐性的同时又能尽量减少由于某种变通而对原诗诗意可能造成的损伤。由于中英两种语言的巨大差异、坡诗的独特性与我们自身能力的限制，我们深知自己的能力只能做到一定程度，倘若我们现在这个译本能基本上传达坡诗的音乐性与诗意，我们的努力应该也就不算徒劳了。是耶非耶，尚请读者诸君批评指正。

刘象愚

2015年初夏于涿州

2018 年初冬改定于多伦多

ANNABEL LEE

It was many and many a year ago,

In a kingdom by the sea,

That a maiden there lived whom you may know

By the name of Annabel Lee;

And this maiden she lived with no other thought

Than to love and be loved by me.

I was a child and she was a child,

In this kingdom by the sea;

But we loved with a love that was more than love —

I and my Annabel Lee;

With a love that the winged seraphs of heaven

Coveted her and me.

And this was the reason that, long ago,

In this kingdom by the sea,

A wind blew out of a cloud, chilling

My beautiful Annabel Lee;

So that her highborn kinsman came

And bore her away from me,

To shut her up in a sepulchre

In this kingdom by the sea.

The angels, not half so happy in heaven,

Went envying her and me —

Yes! — that was the reason (as all men know,

In this kingdom by the sea)

That the wind came out of the cloud by night,

Chilling and killing my Annabel Lee.

But our love it was stronger by far than the love

Of those who were older than we —

Of many far wiser than we —

And neither the angels in heaven above,

Nor the demons down under the sea,

Can ever dissever my soul from the soul

Of the beautiful Annabel Lee.

For the moon never beams without bringing me dreams

Of the beautiful Annabel Lee;

And the stars never rise, but I feel the bright eyes

Of the beautiful Annabel Lee;

And so, all the night-tide, I lie down by the side

Of my darling — my darling — my life and my bride,

In the sepulchre there by the sea,

In her tomb by the sounding sea.

安娜贝儿·李[1]

那是很多，很多年以前，

在海边的一个王国里，

住着一位也许你认识的女孩，

她的名字叫安娜贝儿·李；

这女孩生前没有别的愿望，

爱我，被我爱是她唯一的心事。

那时我是个孩子，她也是个孩子，

在这海边的王国里，

我俩以超越爱的爱相爱，

我和我的安娜贝儿·李——

我们那样相爱，连天上的六翼天使

对她和我也不免觊觎。

而正因了这样的原因，很久以前，

在这海边的王国里，

一阵寒风起自天际，吹冷了

我美丽的安娜贝儿·李；

于是她出身高贵的亲戚前来，

从我身边把她带去，

把她关进地下的石窟，

在这海边的王国里。

天使们一点也不比我们快乐，

对她和我一直心存妒意，

不错！这正是人所共知的原因，

在这海边的王国里，

一阵寒风起自天际，在暗夜里，

冻死了我的安娜贝儿·李。

可我俩的爱远超过人们的爱，

无论是与我们的长辈相比，

还是与那些更聪明的人相比——

不管是飞翔在天堂的天使，

还是游荡在海底的鬼蜮，

都永远不能把我俩的灵魂分开，

我和我美丽的安娜贝儿·李。

只要月光闪现，我就会梦见

我美丽的安娜贝儿·李；

只要星星上升，我就会感到那亮丽的眼神

出自我美丽的安娜贝儿·李；

于是，整个夜晚，我都躺在她身边，

在我的爱——爱，我的生命，我的新娘身边，

在海边她的石窟里，

在呼啸的海边她的坟墓里。

.

THE VALLEY OF UNREST

Once it smiled a silent dell

Where the people did not dwell;

They had gone unto the wars,

Trusting to the mild-eyed stars,

Nightly from their azure towers,

To keep watch above the flowers,

In the midst of which all day

The red sunlight lazily lay.

Now each visitor shall confess

The sad valley's restlessness.

Nothing there is motionless—

Nothing save the airs that brood

Over the magic solitude.

Ah, by no wind are stirred those trees

That palpitate like the chill seas

Around the misty Hebrides!

Ah, by no wind those clouds are driven

That rustle through the unquiet Heaven

Uneasily, from morn till even,

Over the violets there that lie

In myriad types of the human eye—

Over the lilies there that wave

And weep above a nameless grave!

They wave:—from out their fragrant tops

Eternal dews come down in drops.

They weep:—from off their delicate stems

Perennial tears descend in gems.

不安的山谷 [1]

那静谷曾是微笑的净土
人们不曾在那里居住；
他们参加过许多战争，
信任那慈眉善目的星辰，
夜从天蓝色塔顶泻下，
俯瞰着漫山遍野的鲜花，
在万花丛中从早到晚
鲜红的阳光懒散地流连。
而今每一位游客坦言
这悲哀的山谷躁动不安。
没有什么静止不动——
只有空气笼罩着山谷
这充满魔幻的孤独。
哦，没有风把树木搅动
犹如多雾的群岛周边
冰冷的海水那般震颤！
哦，没有风把白云驱赶
犹如天国中的骚乱

整天不安地四处飘散，

在紫罗兰的上方隐伏

仿佛无以数计的人眼——

在百合上波涛般漂浮

在一个无名墓上哭诉！

他们漂浮：从芬芳的花顶

滴下长流不断的露珠。

他们哭诉：从纤弱的花茎

滴落宝石般无尽的泪珠。

1 　此诗写想象中的墓园景象。最早发表于1831年，原名为《尼斯山谷》，1845年发表改用现名。

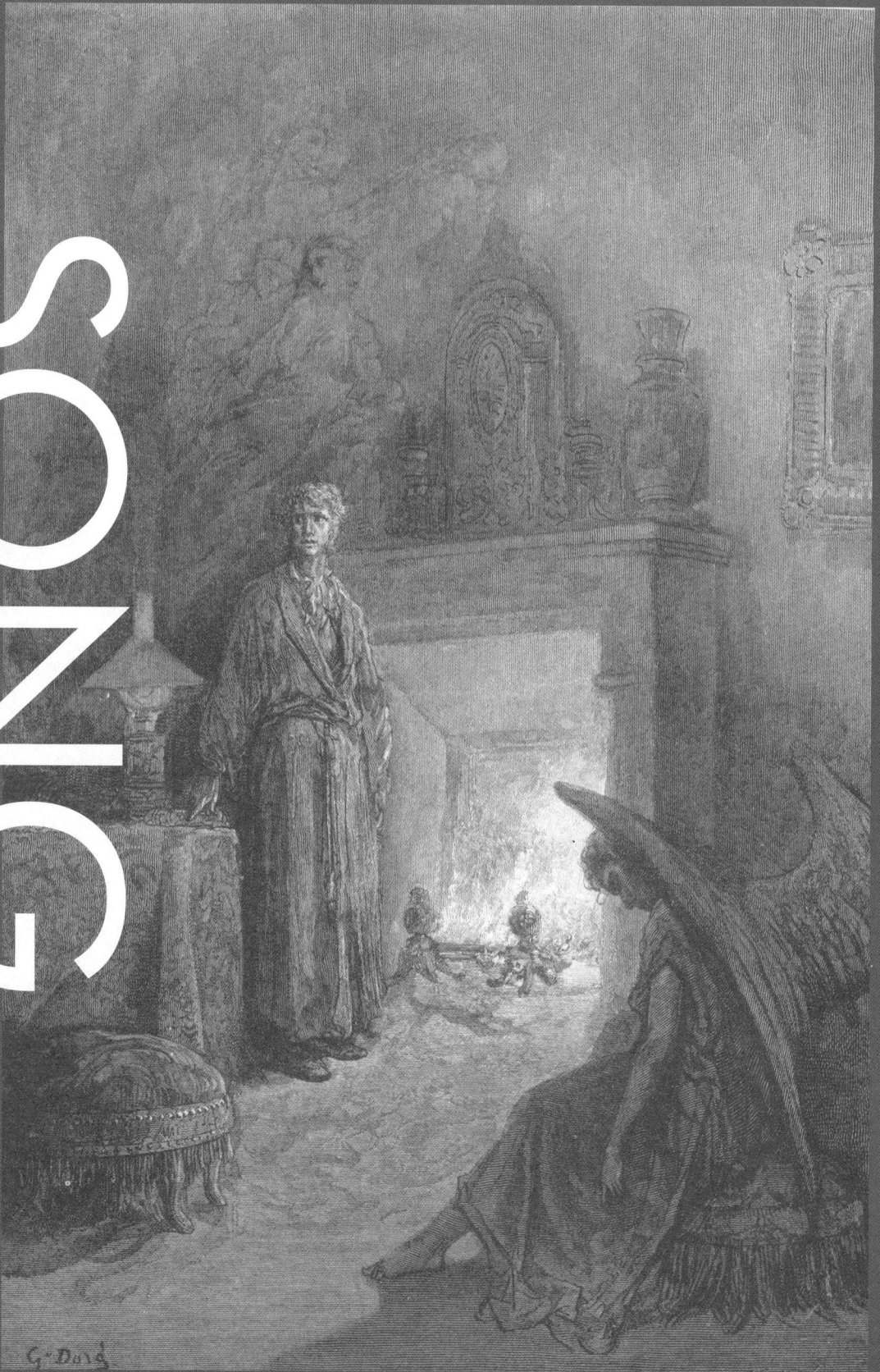

SONG

G. Doré

I saw thee on thy bridal day —

When a burning blush came o'er thee,

Though happiness around thee lay,

The world all love before thee:

And in thine eye a kindling light

(Whatever it might be)

Was all on Earth my aching sight

Of Loveliness could see.

That blush, perhaps, was maiden shame —

As such it well may pass —

Though its glow hath raised a fiercer flame

In the breast of him, alas!

Who saw thee on that bridal day,

When that deep blush would come o'er thee,

Though happiness around thee lay,

The world all love before thee.

歌 [1]

你做新娘那天我看见你——

你满脸飞红，喜气洋溢，

你的周围幸福环绕，

人间的爱都给了你：

你眼中燃烧炽热的光亮

（无论它可能是什么）

全都是我痛苦的目光，

凝聚我爱你的忧伤。

那脸红许是少女的羞惭——

很快就不再显现——

那显现在他爱你的胸中，

天哪！激起更猛的火焰！

你做新娘那天他看见你，

你满脸飞红，喜气洋溢，

你的周围幸福环绕，

人间的爱都给了你。

---

1   此作收入1827年的《帖木儿与其他》中，用歌谣体。一般认为，诗中的新娘指坡少年时代
     的初恋对象莎拉·爱尔米拉·罗伊斯特。莎拉的父亲嫌贫爱富，反对女儿与坡往来，最终将
     女儿嫁与一富家公子。

THE COLISEUM

Type of the antique Rome! Rich reliquary

Of lofty contemplation left to Time

By buried centuries of pomp and power!

At length — at length — after so many days

Of weary pilgrimage and burning thirst,

(Thirst for the springs of lore that in thee lie)

I kneel, an altered and a humble man,

Amid thy shadows, and so drink within

My very soul thy grandeur, gloom, and glory!

Vastness!and Age! and Memories of Eld!

Silence! and Desolation! and dim Night!

I feel ye now — I feel ye in your strength —

O spells more sure than e'er Judaean king

Taught in the gardens of Gethsemane!

O charms more potent than the rapt Chaldee

Ever drew down from out the quiet stars!

Here, where a hero fell, a column falls!

Here, where the mimic eagle glared in gold,

A midnight vigil holds the swarthy bat!

Here, where the dames of Rome their gilded hair

Waved to the wind, now wave the reed and thistle!

Here, where on golden throne the monarch lolled,

Glides, spectre-like, unto his marble home,

Lit by the wan light of the horned moon,

The swift and silent lizard of the stones!

But stay! these walls — these ivy-clad arcades —

These moldering plinths — these sad and blackened shafts —

These vague entablatures — this crumbling frieze —

These shattered cornices — this wreck — this ruin —

These stones — alas! these grey stones — are they all —

All of the famed, and the colossal left

By the corrosive Hours to Fate and me?

"Not all" — the Echoes answer me — "not all!

Prophetic sounds and loud, arise forever

From us, and from all Ruin, unto the wise,

As melody from Memnon to the Sun.

We rule the hearts of mightiest men — we rule

With a despotic sway all giant minds.

We are not impotent — we pallid stones.

Not all our power is gone — not all our fame —

Not all the magic of our high renown —

Not all the wonder that encircles us —

Not all the mysteries that in us lie —

Not all the memories that hang upon

And cling around about us as a garment,

Clothing us in a robe of more than glory."

古罗马竞技场¹

古罗马的象征！被无数世纪的

辉煌和权力遗留给时光

令人沉思的丰厚圣物！

终于——终于——经历了许多时日

疲乏的朝圣，燃烧着渴望，

（渴望探求你深藏的传说宝藏）

我，一个改变了的、谦卑的人，

跪在你的阴影里，我的灵魂

深深吮吸你的辉煌、忧郁和荣光！

广袤啊！悠久啊！古代的记忆！

沉默啊！荒凉啊！黑暗的夜！

此刻我感到了你——感到了你的力量——

那是怎样的魔幻呀，胜过犹太王

客西马尼花园²中的教诲！

那是怎样的魅力呀，胜过迦勒底人³

从静默星球入迷地汲取的精髓！

这里一根圆柱坍塌，就有一个英雄倒下！

这里黄金仿制的雄鹰曾怒视，

而今黑黢黢的蝙蝠却警戒着午夜！

这里罗马贵妇们金色的长发曾随风

飘曳，而今飘曳的却是芦苇和荆棘！

这里君王曾瘫坐在黄金宝座上，

而今在角状月牙的苍白幽光下，

幽灵般滑进他大理石家园的却是

迅疾沉默地爬行在石上的蜥蜴！

可是且慢！这些垣壁、爬满青藤的拱门——

这些腐朽的基座——伤心变黑的廊柱——

这些模糊的柱顶线盘——这不断碎裂的带饰——

这些四分五裂的飞檐——这残迹——这废墟——

这些石头，天哪！这些灰白的石头，难道它们都是——

都是*岁月*侵蚀下显赫的名声和宏伟的人事

遗留，遗留给*命运之神*和我的陈迹？

"不然"，回声回答我，"不然！

先知般的声音，大声地、永久地响起

从我们心里，从所有废墟，向智者，

有如美妙的旋律，从曼侬向太阳响起[4]。

我们统治最强伟人的心，用专制力量

统治所有那些巨人们的心灵。

我们并非无能——我们这些苍白的石头。

我们的力量并未全部丧失——我们所有的令名——

我们巨大荣耀的魅力——

环绕我们的所有奇迹——

我们深藏内心的所有神秘——

那些所有紧紧粘着我们，长袍大褂般

裹紧我们，将我们包裹在远大于

荣耀中的记忆，并未全部丧失。"

1   此作发表于1833年10月26日《巴尔的摩星期六游客报》，是参加诗歌竞赛的获奖作品。此
     作不注重尾韵，诗律不一。坡认为这是他最好的作品之一。
2   耶路撒冷城外橄榄山的一座花园，耶稣在犹大背叛他之后曾在这里祈祷。
3   古代两河流域的迦勒底王国或称巴比伦王国，迦勒底人擅长占星术，故这里也可引申为星
     相学家。
4   这里的典故似指3500年前尼罗河西岸埃及法老阿蒙豪特的两尊巨大石像，由于后来的剧
     烈地震石像从腰部震断，传说这毁坏的下半截石像在黎明太阳光的照射下会发出美妙的
     音响。

THE CITY IN THE SEA

Lo! Death has reared himself a throne

In a strange city lying alone

Far down within the dim West,

Where the good and the bad and the worst and the best

Have gone to their eternal rest.

There shrines and palaces and towers

(Time-eaten towers that tremble not!)

Resemble nothing that is ours.

Around, by lifting winds forgot,

Resignedly beneath the sky

The melancholy waters lie.

No rays from the holy heaven come down

On the long night-time of that town;

But light from out the lurid sea

Streams up the turrets silently —

Gleams up the pinnacles far and free —

Up domes — up spires — up kingly halls —

Up fanes — up Babylon-like walls —

Up shadowy long-forgotten bowers

Of sculptured ivy and stone flowers —

Up many and many a marvellous shrine

Whose wreathed friezes intertwine

The viol, the violet, and the vine.

Resignedly beneath the sky

The melancholy waters lie.

So blend the turrets and shadows there

That all seem pendulous in air,

While from a proud tower in the town

Death looks gigantically down.

There open fanes and gaping graves

Yawn level with the luminous waves;

But not the riches there that lie

In each idol's diamond eye —

Not the gaily-jewelled dead

Tempt the waters from their bed;

For no ripples curl, alas!

Along that wilderness of glass —

No swellings tell that winds may be

Upon some far-off happier sea —

No heavings hint that winds have been

On seas less hideously serene.

But lo, a stir is in the air!

The wave — there is a movement there!

As if the towers had thrust aside,

In slightly sinking, the dull tide —

As if their tops had feebly given

A void within the filmy Heaven.

The waves have now a redder glow —

The hours are breathing faint and low —

And when, amid no earthly moans,

Down, down that town shall settle hence,

Hell, rising from a thousand thrones,

Shall do it reverence.

海中的城市 [1]

看哪！死神为自己建了一座殿堂

在一个古怪的城市，寂寞凄凉，

遥远地，在幽暗的西边，

那儿，恶与善，至恶与至善

全都进入永恒的休眠。

那里的神龛、宫殿和尖塔

（在时间侵蚀中不再摇晃！）

和我们这里的形成巨大反差。

而四周，被掀浪的大风遗忘，

在天空下毫无生气地沉睡

是一片忧郁悲怆的海水。

没有任何光辉洒自圣洁的苍穹

照耀在这漫漫长夜的城中；

只有幽光从森冷闪烁的海面，

静默无声地漫上塔楼顶尖——

从四面八方涌上角塔尖端——

爬上穹顶——尖顶——皇家的厅堂——

爬上寺庙——巴比伦式的宫墙——

爬上早被弃置的阴暗的凉厅——

厅中的石花和雕刻的青藤——

爬上许许多多奇异的神龛

那柱顶墙头雕饰的花环

缠绕着古提琴、葡萄藤和紫罗兰。

在天空下毫无生气地沉睡

是一片忧郁悲怆的海水。

塔楼和阴影混溶在水中

仿佛一切都悬浮在天空,

而在城中一座高塔之上

庞大的死神正傲视着下方。

那里敞开的寺庙和裂开的坟茔

大张着嘴,和闪烁的海水持平;

每一座偶像的钻石眼珠

蕴含着的全部财富——

所有珠光宝气的死尸,

都无法引诱海水涌起;

哦,因为没有碎浪微澜

沿着那玻璃的荒原震颤,

没有膨胀显示海水也许

在稍微明快的远海掀起——

没有起伏暗示风浪曾经

打破那不太狰狞的宁静。

可是看哪！一阵骚动起于空中！

波浪在海上生了一丝涌动！

仿佛那些塔楼在微微下坠

已经在推开死寂的潮水——

仿佛那些尖顶已经无力地放弃

它们在朦胧天上的位置。

海水此刻放出更深的红光——

时间的呼吸只有低弱的声响——

于是此城在此地下沉，下沉，

再也没有了任何尘世的呻吟，

地狱从千百个宝座上升，

向着这沉沦的城市致敬。

THE LAKE —TO

IN spring of youth it was my lot

To haunt of the wide world a spot

The which I could not love the less —

So lovely was the loneliness

Of a wild lake, with black rock bound,

And the tall pines that towered around.

But when the Night had thrown her pall

Upon that spot, as upon all,

And the mystic wind went by

Murmuring in melody —

Then — ah then I would awake

To the terror of the lone lake.

Yet that terror was not fright,

But a tremulous delight —

A feeling not the jeweled mine

Could teach or bribe me to define —

Nor Love — although the Love were thine.

Death was in that poisonous wave,

And in its gulf a fitting grave

For him who thence could solace bring

To his lone imagining —

Whose solitary soul could make

An Eden of that dim lake.

湖——致¹

青春岁月里我的命运

势必在广袤世界追寻

我极端热爱的地方——

它的孤独令我向往，

那是荒野的湖，黑石环绕，

高大的苍松耸入云霄。

可每当*夜神*垂下尸衣

湖上和四周一片死寂，

神秘的风从耳边吹过

发出絮絮叨叨的旋律——

于是我悚然醒来，

面对孤独的湖的恐惧。

然而那恐惧并非惊骇，

却是战栗不止的欢快——

一种难以言传的感情

宝藏也不能贿赂我说清——

即使你的爱也无法辨明。

死神在剧毒的波涛中驻足，
它的港湾恰恰是适宜的坟墓
可以带给他宁静与慰藉
安抚他孤独的想象力——
他孤独的灵魂于是浮想联翩
使这阴郁的湖成为他的乐园。

1　这首诗首发于1827年，原题《湖》，1829年改作《湖——致》。

Ah, broken is the golden bowl! the spirit flown forever!

Let the bell toll! — a saintly soul floats on the Stygian river;

And, Guy de Vere, hast thou no tear? — weep now or nevermore!

See! on yon drear and rigid bier low lies thy love, Lenore!

Come! let the burial rite be read — the funeral song be sung! —

An anthem for the queenliest dead that ever died so young —

A dirge for her the doubly dead in that she died so young.

"Wretches! ye loved her for her wealth and hated her for her pride,

And when she fell in feeble health, ye blessed her — that she died!

How shall the ritual, then, be read? — the requiem how be sung

By you — by yours, the evil eye, — by yours, the slanderous tongue

That did to death the innocence that died, and died so young?"

Peccavimus; but rave not thus! and let a Sabbath song

Go up to God so solemnly the dead may feel no wrong.

The sweet Lenore hath "gone before", with Hope, that flew beside,

Leaving thee wild for the dear child that should have been thy bride—

For her, the fair and debonair, that now so lowly lies,

The life upon her yellow hair but not within her eyes —

The life still there, upon her hair — the death upon her eyes.

"Avaunt! avaunt! from fiends below, the indignant ghost is riven—

From Hell unto a high estate far up within the Heaven-

From grief and groan, to a golden throne, beside the King of Heaven!

Let no bell toll, then,—lest her soul, amid its hallowed mirth,

Should catch the note as it doth float up from the damned Earth!

And I !—to-night my heart is light!—no dirge will I upraise,

But waft the angel on her flight with a Paean of old days!"

莱诺儿 [1]

哦，金碗打碎了！精灵永恒飞翔！

让丧钟敲响！——一个圣洁的灵魂漂浮在冥河上；

盖蒂·维尔，你没有泪吗？——那么，哭吧，不然就不再！

看呀！那边冷硬的棺架上悲凉地躺着莱诺儿，你的心爱。

来吧，让葬礼开始——让挽歌唱起！

哀悼如此年轻的女王般的死——

为了她如此年轻的双重的死的葬仪。

"可怜的人！你爱她的财富——却恨她的骄傲，

当她一病不起，你为她祝福——使她陨凋！

那么，你，你眼神邪恶——你毒舌伤人，

将怎样去做葬礼？怎样唱安魂弥撒——

怎样对待那天真烂漫的死，那夭折的亡魂？"

我们深悔罪重；别那么胡说！且把安息曲唱起

对上帝严肃地悔罪，让亡灵不再含冤孤凄。

心爱的莱诺儿已经"逝世"，与希望一道消亡，

让你发狂，这亲爱的人原应是你的新娘——

052

她是那般美丽文雅，可此刻却静卧不起，那般死寂，

她的金发依旧生动，她的眼已经了无声息——

生命在她的发上，可死亡在她的眼里。

"滚吧！滚吧！从地下恶魔、被撕裂的恶魂——

从地狱到天国中高高在上的圣人身份——

从悲伤哀泣到天国之王的金色宝座旁！

再不能让丧钟敲响！——以免她的灵魂在圣洁的欢乐中，

听到这该死的，从地下飘出的丧钟！

而我！——我的心今晚已轻松，不再把挽歌唱响，

让我的天使与我往昔的赞歌一起飞翔！"

---

1   这首诗首发于1831年，原题《赞歌》，1843与1845年改作现题，内容也做了较大的改动。
    此作仍采用"美人的早逝"这一诗人惯用的主题。此作不仅有很强的音乐性，也有很强的
    戏剧性，第一、三两节是"叙述者"的话；而第二、四两节是莱诺儿的恋人盖蒂·维尔的
    话，所以放在引号中。

Romance, who loves to nod and sing,

With drowsy head and folded wing,

Among the green leaves as they shake

Far down within some shadowy lake,

To me a painted paroquet

Hath been — a most familiar bird —

Taught me my alphabet to say —

To lisp my very earliest word

While in the wild wood I did lie,

A child — with a most knowing eye.

Of late, eternal Condor years

So shake the very Heaven on high

With tumult as they thunder by,

I have no time for idle cares

Through gazing on the unquiet sky.

And when an hour with calmer wings

Its down upon my spirit flings —

That little time with lyre and rhyme

To while away — forbidden things !

My heart would feel to be a crime

Unless it trembled with the strings.

浪漫女神 [1]

浪漫女神，你爱打盹和歌唱，

困倦的头低垂，收起翅膀，

在随风摇曳的绿树丛中

山下绿荫扶疏的湖面上，

你是人们最熟知的鸟儿

我心目中彩色的鹦鹉，

你教我说话认字——

咿呀吐出最早的言词

那时我躺在原始老林，

有着孩童般求知的眼神。

随后岁月永恒雄鹰奋起

搏击长空，震撼天庭

掀起波澜，发动雷霆，

我再无暇作懒散的遐思

对着不平静的天空凝视。

有时偶尔双翅沉稳平静

降临我不安的心灵——

我用音乐和诗消磨时间

唱出禁锢心中的幽情!

我的心会有一种负罪感

除非它与琴弦一起颤动。

1　此作最早收入1829年的《艾尔·阿拉夫、帖木儿与其他》中，原名《序言》，1831年再次收入诗集中时改名为《引言》，1843年始改作现名。原诗与现在这个文本有比较大的差异。诗中所谓的"浪漫女神"暗指诗人心仪和爱过的女性。

A DREAM

In visions of the dark night

I have dreamed of joy departed;

But a waking dream of life and light

Hath left me broken-hearted.

Ah! what is not a dream by day

To him whose eyes are cast

On things around him, with a ray

Turned back upon the past?

That holy dream, that holy dream,

While all the world were chiding,

Hath cheered me as a lovely beam

A lonely spirit guiding.

What though that light, thro' storm and night,

So trembled from afar —

What could there be more purely bright

In Truth's day-star?

梦¹

沉沉暗夜的幻象中
我梦见逝去的喜悦；
而光天化日醒着的梦
却把我的心儿撕裂。

哦！白日梦不是梦境，
他的眼睛闪着亮光，
环顾周围事物和情景，
一切都转回到以往。

那神圣的梦啊，神圣的梦，
有如可爱的光束让我兴奋，
当整个世界充满指责声，
它引导我孤独的心灵前行。

那亮光穿越风暴与暗夜，
来自遥远，震颤不已——
倘若*真实*的白昼星辰有更多
纯净的辉光，该是何等欣喜？

1   此作1827年收入《帖木儿及其他》中，没有诗题；1829年再次收入诗集时增加了现在的标
     题。诗人对比了夜梦与白日梦（即现实），如今现实中的悲惨与失意让他更愿意进入以往
     夜梦的喜悦中。

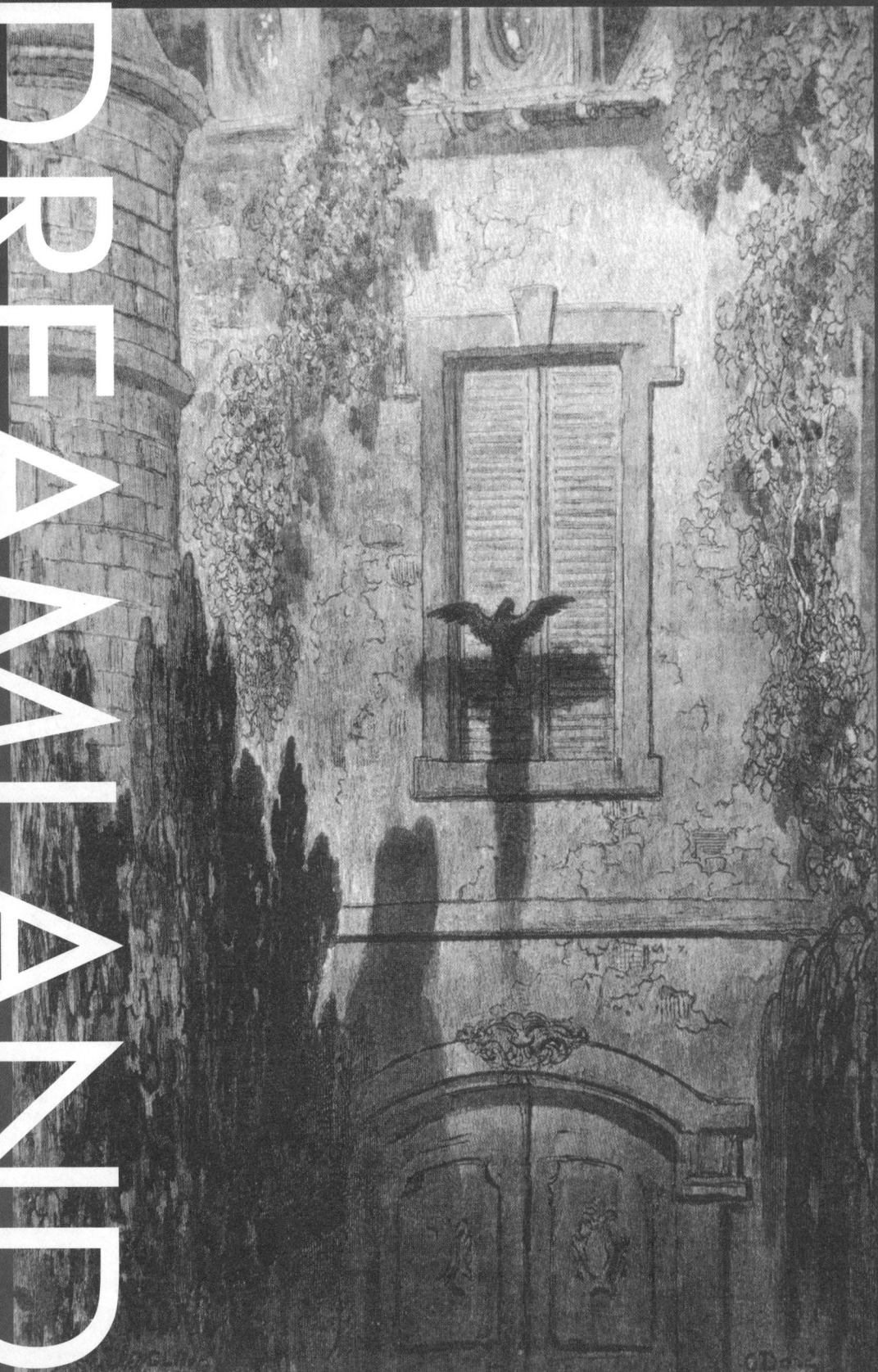

DREAMLAND

By a route obscure and lonely,

Haunted by ill angels only,

Where an Eidolon, named Night,

On a black throne reigns upright,

I have reached these lands but newly

From an ultimate dim Thule —

From a wild clime that lieth, sublime,

Out of Space — out of Time.

Bottomless vales and boundless floods,

And chasms, and caves, and Titan woods,

With forms that no man can discover

For the tears that drip all over;

Mountains toppling evermore

Into seas without a shore;

Seas that restlessly aspire,

Surging, unto skies of fire;

Lakes that endlessly outspread

Their lone waters — lone and dead, —

Their still waters — still and chilly

With the snows of the lolling lily.

By the lakes that thus outspread

Their lone waters, lone and dead, —

Their sad waters, sad and chilly

With the snows of the lolling lily, —

By the mountains — near the river

Murmuring lowly, murmuring ever, —

By the gray woods, — by the swamp

Where the toad and the newt encamp —

By the dismal tarns and pools

Where dwell the Ghouls, —

By each spot the most unholy —

In each nook most melancholy —

There the traveler meets aghast

Sheeted Memories of the Past —

Shrouded forms that start and sigh

As they pass the wanderer by —

White-robed forms of friends long given,

In agony, to the Earth — and Heaven.

For the heart whose woes are legion

'Tis a peaceful, soothing region —

For the spirit that walks in shadow

'Tis — oh, 'tis an Eldorado!

But the traveler, travelling through it,

May not — dare not openly view it!

Never its mysteries are exposed

To the weak human eye unclosed;

So wills its King, who hath forbid

The uplifting of the fringed lid;

And thus the sad Soul that here passes

Beholds it but through darkened glasses.

By a route obscure and lonely,

Haunted by ill angels only,

Where an Eidolon, named Night,

On a black throne reigns upright,

I have wandered home but newly

From this ultimate dim Thule.

梦境 [1]

一条路晦暗又孤独，

只有邪恶天使出入，

一个称作*夜*的*幽灵*，

高踞黑宝座发号施令，

我刚刚来到这里

从阴暗的世外*极地*——

那是一片肃穆的荒原，

超越*空间*——超越*时间*。

峡谷无底，洪水无涯，

*巨人般*森林、洞穴、断崖，

没人见过这般形状

泪水纵横遮没一切景象；

群山在不停崩溃

落入无边的海水；

海洋躁动不安地翻腾，

涌上烈火熊熊的苍穹；

湖泊无休止向外扩展

湖水孤独——孤独死寂——

湖水静止——静止寒彻

伴着萎靡百合花般的雪。

湖就这样向外扩展

湖水孤独,孤独死寂——

湖水悲凉,悲凉寒彻

伴着萎靡百合花般的雪——

依傍群山——靠近河流

河流低诉,不停怨尤——

靠着灰暗森林——连着沼泽

那是蟾蜍和蝾螈的营地——

阴沉的冰斗湖和池塘

那是食尸鬼居住的地方——

在最不神圣的每一处所——

在最阴郁的每一角落——

旅人被这般景象惊呆,

往昔记忆在尸衣中展开——

尸衣中的形体个个惊起

从旅人眼前通过,叹息——

早已逝去的故人白袍裹身,

极度痛苦,走向*尘世*和*天庭*。

对于被剧痛压垮的身心，

这里安宁，充满慰欣——

对于暗影里行走的灵魂

这里——哦，就是黄金国度！

可旅人，到这里旅行，

却不能——也不敢睁开眼睛！

它的神秘永不展现

在虚弱的世人眼前；

它君王的意志盒子禁开

神秘而布满饰带的盖；

由此经过的可悲魂灵

只能用深色镜观看此景。

一条路晦暗又孤独，

只有邪恶天使出入，

一个称作*夜*的*幽灵*，

高踞黑宝座发号施令，

我刚游历回到家里

离开这阴暗的世外极地。

Take this kiss upon the brow!

And, in parting from you now,

Thus much let me avow —

You are not wrong, who deem

That my days have been a dream;

Yet if hope has flown away

In a night, or in a day,

In a vision, or in none,

Is it therefore the less gone?

All that we see or seem

Is but a dream within a dream.

I stand amid the roar

Of a surf-tormented shore,

And I hold within my hand

Grains of the golden sand —

How few! yet how they creep

Through my fingers to the deep,

While I weep — while I weep!

O God! can I not grasp

Them with a tighter clasp?

O God! can I not save

One from the pitiless wave?

Is all that we see or seem

But a dream within a dream?

梦中梦¹

请接受你额上的这一吻！
在我们分别的时辰，
让我就此向你承认——
你没有错，你宣称
我的过去是一场梦；
然而如果希望飞散
无论夜晚，或者白天，
无论幻觉，或者知晓，
难道失去的会更少？
我们看到或认为的一切
只不过是一场梦中梦。

我站在喧嚣的海边
波涛翻腾的海岸，
我手中紧紧抓起
黄金沙子的颗粒—
多么少啊！沙粒怎样
从我指缝流向大海深处，

我心哀伤——不禁痛哭！

哦，上帝！难道我无力

将它们更紧地抓在手里？

哦，上帝！难道我无法

把一粒沙从无情的波涛留下？

难道我们看到或认为的一切

都只能是一场梦中梦？

1　此作发表于1849年，也即诗人逝世那年。诗作表达一种人生如梦的主题。

THE HAUNTED PALACE

In the greenest of our valleys

By good angels tenanted,

Once a fair and stately palace —

Radiant palace — reared its head.

In the monarch Thought's dominion —

It stood there!

Never seraph spread a pinion

Over fabric half so fair!

Banners yellow, glorious, golden,

On its roof did float and flow,

(This — all this — was in the olden Time long ago,)

And every gentle air that dallied,

In that sweet day,

Along the ramparts plumed and pallid,

A wingéd odor went away.

Wanderers in that happy valley,

Through two luminous windows, saw

Spirits moving musically,

To a lute's well-tunéd law,

Round about a throne where, sitting

(Porphyrogene!)

In state his glory well befitting,

The ruler of the realm was seen.

And all with pearl and ruby glowing

Was the fair palace door,

Through which came flowing, flowing, flowing,

And sparkling evermore,

A troop of Echoes, whose sweet duty

Was but to sing,

In voices of surpassing beauty,

The wit and wisdom of their king.

But evil things, in robes of sorrow,

Assailed the monarch's high estate.

(Ah, let us mourn! — for never morrow

Shall dawn upon him desolate!)

And round about his home the glory

That blushed and bloomed,

Is but a dim-remembered story

Of the old time entombed.

And travelers, now, within that valley,

Through the red-litten windows see

Vast forms, that move fantastically

To a discordant melody,

While, like a ghastly rapid river,

Through the pale door

A hideous throng rush out forever

And laugh — but smile no more.

闹鬼的宫殿 ¹

我们青葱无比的山谷

被善良的天使租住，

曾经美丽庄严的宫殿——

辉煌灿烂——高昂着头颅。

在思想统治的王国里，

这宫殿曾巍然挺立！

天使展示美丽翅膀，

从未见有它一半的美丽！

黄色的旗，金碧辉煌，

在它屋顶随风飘扬，

（这一切都属于遥远古老的往昔时光）

每一缕柔和的气息，

曾在甜美日子嬉戏，

沿着苍白的羽饰护墙，

羽翼的气味飘散远方。

这快乐山谷的游人，

透过两扇闪光的窗

看到精灵轻快来去，

和着诗琴美妙的旋律，

这个王国的君王

（好一派皇家气象！）

雄踞那边的宝座，

威风十足，至高无上。

宫殿大门气势宏伟

镶满珠宝无限精美

从这里不息地流入哟，

是永远闪耀的光辉，

那是回声女神的大军，

美好的职责就是歌唱，

用魅力无穷的歌喉，

把君王的英明颂扬。

可恶魔披着悲情长袍，

袭击了王国的首脑。

（哦，让我们哀悼！哀悼

他已不再有明天的破晓！）

娇羞怒放的荣光

曾在他的故乡传扬，

而今已是被埋葬的往日

依稀难辨的故事。

此刻，山谷中的游人，

透过红光闪烁的窗看见

硕大的形体伴着噪音

古怪地来来去去，

丑恶的一群不断冲出

犹如一条鬼影的急流，

穿过宫殿苍白的大门

狞笑着——可微笑再也没有。

---

1   此作1839年4月发表于《美国博物馆》杂志上，后引入其短篇小说《厄舍古屋的崩塌》中，
     被主人公厄舍吟唱。此作以"闹鬼的宫殿"象征精神错乱的头脑，前四节着力写从前的辉
     煌壮丽，后两节笔锋一转，写在恐怖外力笼罩的当下，宫殿被魑魅魍魉控制的情节。

HYMN

AT morn — at noon — at twilight dim —

Maria! thou hast heard my hymn!

In joy and woe — in good and ill —

Mother of God, be with me still!

When the Hours flew brightly by,

And not a cloud obscured the sky,

My soul, lest it should truant be,

Thy grace did guide to thine and thee ;

Now, when storms of Fate o'ercast

Darkly my Present and my Past,

Let my Future radiant shine

With sweet hopes of thee and thine!

圣母颂 [1]

清晨——正午——薄暮的昏黄——

玛丽亚！您听见我赞美的歌唱！

无论快乐忧伤——无论生病健康——

圣母啊，愿您永远在我身旁！

当*时光*在我身边欢快溜过，

晴空万里没有一丝云朵，

您的恩爱引我靠近您身边，

以免我的灵魂怠惰懒散；

此刻，*命运*的暴风骤雨

遮蔽了我的*现在*和过去，

愿您和您的美好希望

让我的*未来*闪耀光芒！

1   这首对圣母的颂歌1835年首次出现在短篇小说《莫瑞拉》中，原本16行，后来独立发表，
减作12行，两句一韵。

SONNET — TO SCIENCE

Science! true daughter of Old Time thou art!

Who alterest all things with thy peering eyes.

Why preyest thou thus upon the poet's heart,

Vulture, whose wings are dull realities?

How should he love thee? or how deem thee wise?

Who wouldst not leave him in his wandering

To seek for treasure in the jeweled skies,

Albeit he soared with an undaunted wing?

Hast thou not dragged Diana from her car?

And driven the Hamadryad from the wood

To seek a shelter in some happier star?

Hast thou not torn the Naiad from her flood,

The Elfin from the green grass, and from me

The summer dream beneath the tamarind tree?

十四行诗——致科学 ¹

科学啊！你这*时光老人忠诚的女儿*！

你用凝视的目光改变一切人事。

可你为何要这般攫食诗人的心儿，

兀鹰啊，难道你的翅膀是阴暗的现实？

他怎能爱你？或把你看作高明的代表？

是谁不肯让他在人间自在游荡，

不肯让他在钻石的天空探奇寻宝，

纵然他拍击无畏的翅膀高翔？

难道你没有把*狄安娜*²拖下马车？

没有把*哈马德娅*³赶出山林家园，

让她们去某颗幸运的星球寻找房舍？

难道你没有把*妮娅德*⁴拽出山泉，

把小精灵赶出绿色草场，不曾

从罗望子树下撕裂我夏日的梦？

1   此作首发于1829年。诗人对现代科学对艺术和人的精神造成的危害深感忧虑。

2   罗马神话中的狩猎与月亮女神。

3   希腊罗马神话中的山林女神。

4   希腊神话中的水泽女神。

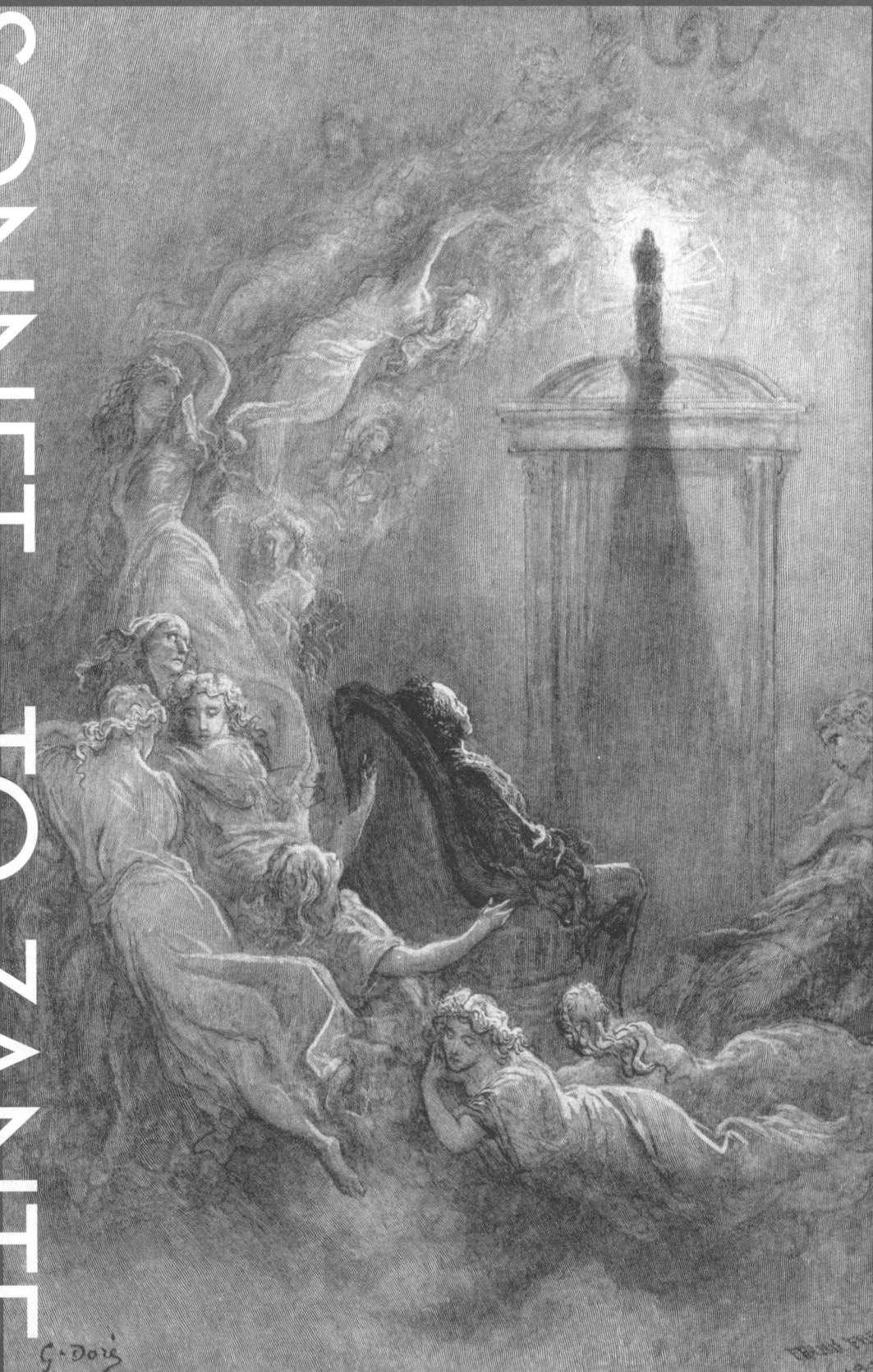

SONNET — TO ZANTE

Fair isle, that from the fairest of all flowers,

Thy gentlest of all gentle names dost take!

How many memories of what radiant hours

At sight of thee and thine at once awake!

How many scenes of what departed bliss!

How many thoughts of what entombéd hopes!

How many visions of a maiden that is

No more — no more upon thy verdant slopes!

No more! alas, that magical sad sound

Transforming all! Thy charms shall please no more!

Thy memory no more! Acccurséd ground

Henceforth I hold thy flower-enamelled shore,

O hyacinthine isle! O purple Zante!

"Isola d'oro! Fior di Levante!"

十四行诗——致桑特岛 [1]

美丽的岛啊，你是鲜花中最美的一朵，

你有所有美名中最美的名字！

见到你的刹那立刻精神振作，

往昔许多美好的时刻顿时记起！

多少次分别的幸福时光再现！

多少次被埋葬的希望在心中跳荡！

多少次幻觉中看到你美丽的容颜

可翠绿的山坡上再也见不到你的形象！

再也看不到你奇妙销魂的魅力！

再也听不到你夺人心魄的悲音！

再没有你的记忆！你这该诅咒的土地！

我将抓住你鲜花釉彩的海滨，

哦，风信子岛啊！紫色的桑特岛！

"金色的岛啊！风信子花的岛！" [2]

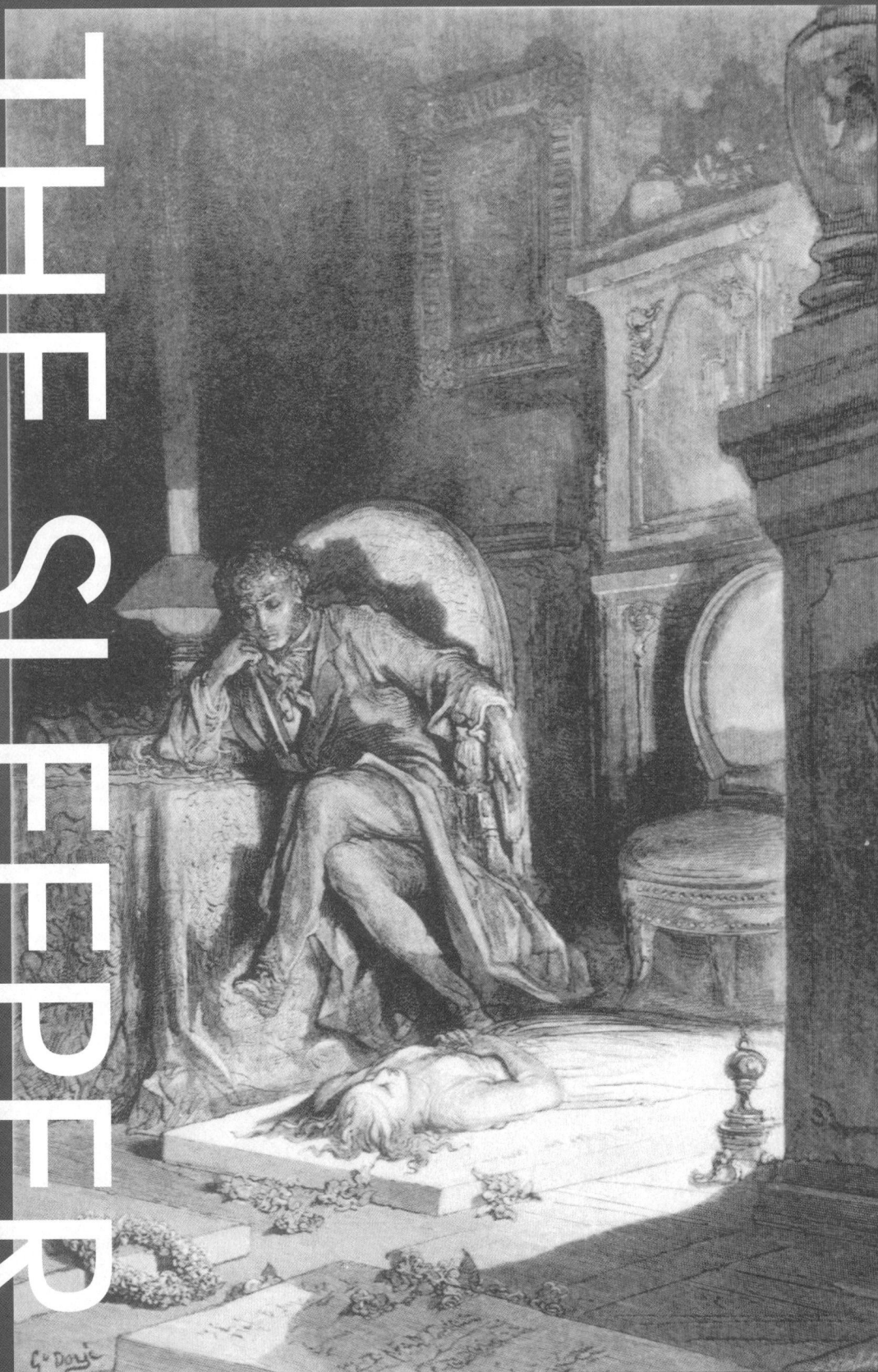

THE SLEEPER

At midnight, in the month of June,

I stand beneath the mystic moon.

An opiate vapor, dewy, dim,

Exhales from out her golden rim,

And, softly dripping, drop by drop,

Upon the quiet mountain top,

Steals drowsily and musically

Into the universal valley.

The rosemary nods upon the grave;

The lily lolls upon the wave;

Wrapping the fog about its breast,

The ruin molders into rest;

Looking like Lethe, see! the lake

A conscious slumber seems to take,

And would not, for the world, awake.

All Beauty sleeps! — and lo! where lies

(Her casement open to the skies)

Irene, with her Destinies!

Oh, lady bright! can it be right —

This window open to the night?

The wanton airs, from the tree-top,

Laughingly through the lattice drop —

The bodiless airs, a wizard rout,

Flit through thy chamber in and out,

And wave the curtain canopy

So fitfully — so fearfully —

Above the closed and fringed lid

Neath which thy slumb'ring soul lies hid,

That o'er the floor and down the wall,

Like ghosts the shadows rise and fall!

Oh, lady dear, hast thou no fear?

Why and what art thou dreaming here?

Sure thou art come o'er far-off seas,

A wonder to these garden trees!

Strange is thy pallor! strange thy dress!

Strange, above all, thy length of tress,

And this all solemn silentness!

The lady sleeps! Oh, may her sleep,

Which is enduring, so be deep!

Heaven have her in its sacred keep!

This chamber changed for one more holy,

This bed for one more melancholy,

I pray to God that she may lie

Forever with unopened eye,

While the dim sheeted ghosts go by!

My love, she sleeps! Oh, may her sleep,

As it is lasting, so be deep!

Soft may the worms about her creep!

Far in the forest, dim and old,

For her may some tall vault unfold —

Some vault that oft hath flung its black

And winged panels fluttering back,

Triumphant, o'er the crested palls,

Of her grand family funerals —

Some sepulchre, remote, alone,

Against whose portal she hath thrown,

In childhood, many an idle stone —

Some tomb from out whose sounding door

She ne'er shall force an echo more,

Thrilling to think, poor child of sin!

It was the dead who groaned within.

睡美人 [1]

那是六月的午夜之际，

我在神秘的月下伫立。

鸦片烟雾的昏暗露珠，

从她金色的边缘呼出，

柔软地，一滴滴滴落，

落在静寂的峰顶山坡，

昏沉地、音乐般溜入，

每一条深山峡谷。

迷迭香向坟墓垂首；

百合花懒倚着浪头；

废墟把雾气揽入胸怀，

溃散地进入休眠状态；

看哪！多像忘川水，

湖泊仿佛在自觉安睡，

无论如何不愿再醒。

看哪！美人全睡了！现在

依莲娜和命运女神并排，

（她的窗扉朝天敞开！）

哦，聪明的夫人！可该让——

这窗扉对暗夜开放？

那淫荡的气流，从树梢

大笑着闯入你的灵窍——

那无形气流，溃败的男巫，

在你闺阁中自由出入，

挥舞华盖般的帘幕，

那般疯癫——那般恐怖——

在你闭合的流苏眼睑上

你沉睡的灵魂在那儿隐藏，

阴影幽灵般升起沉落，

在地上，在墙上出没！

哦，亲爱的夫人，你不怕吗？

你在这儿梦什么，又为什么？

不错，你来自遥远的海上，

奇迹般光临花园的树上！

奇怪，你的苍白！奇怪，你的衣服！

更奇怪的是你美发的长度，

而这一切都沉静肃穆！

那夫人睡了！哦，愿她安眠，

愿她长久、深沉地安眠！

天堂已把她拥入圣殿！

这闺阁已变得更圣洁，

这床已变得更郁结，

我祈祷上帝让她安息

眼睛永恒地紧闭，

一任裹尸衣的幽魂游弋！

我的爱，她已安眠！哦，愿她安眠，

愿她永远、深沉地安眠！

愿她周围的小虫爬得轻慢！

在遥远、阴暗而古老的林中，

愿大墓为她敞开穹窿——

墓穴常开黑色的棺板

黑色的棺板羽翼般震颤，

得意地，拍击彩饰尸衣，

展示她盛大的家族葬仪——

远处一座坟墓孑然独立，

儿时她曾顽皮地嬉戏，

向墓门投掷许多碎石——

如今她再也无力击打墓门

听碎石撞击墓门的回声，

想来令人心惊，可怜的罪人！

那是墓穴中亡灵痛苦的呻吟。

此作首发于1831年，收入当年的诗集中，原题《伊莲娜》，74行，后经多次修改，成为现在的版本。诗作涉及了诗人一贯的主题，即对年轻美丽的女子早逝的伤逝以及关于生死的思考。全诗61行，主要用双行或三行韵。诗人曾说过，此诗是他的佳作之一，甚至比《乌鸦》还好。

TAMERLANE

KIND solace in a dying hour!

Such, father, is not (now) my theme —

I will not madly deem that power

Of Earth may shrive me of the sin

Unearthly pride hath revell'd in —

I have no time to dote or dream:

You call it hope — that fire of fire!

It is but agony of desire:

If I can hope — Oh God! I can —

Its fount is holier — more divine —

I would not call thee fool, old man,

But such is not a gift of thine.

Know thou the secret of a spirit

Bow'd from its wild pride into shame.

O! yearning heart! I did inherit

Thy withering portion with the fame,

The searing glory which hath shone

Amid the jewels of my throne,

Halo of Hell! and with a pain

Not Hell shall make me fear again —

O! craving heart, for the lost flowers

And sunshine of my summer hours!

The undying voice of that dead time,

With its interminable chime,

Rings, in the spirit of a spell,

Upon thy emptiness — a knell.

I have not always been as now:

The fever'd diadem on my brow

I claim'd and won usurpingly —

Hath not the same fierce heirdom given

Rome to the Caesar — this to me?

The heritage of a kingly mind,

And a proud spirit which hath striven

Triumphantly with human kind.

On mountain soil I first drew life:

The mists of the Taglay have shed

Nightly their dews upon my head,

And, I believe, the winged strife

And tumult of the headlong air

Have nestled in my very hair.

So late from Heaven — that dew — it fell

('Mid dreams of an unholy night)

Upon me with the touch of Hell,

While the red flashing of the light

From clouds that hung, like banners, o'er,

Appeared to my half-closing eye

The pageantry of monarchy,

And the deep trumpet-thunder's roar

Came hurriedly upon me, telling

Of human battle, where my voice,

My own voice, silly child! — was swelling

(Oh! how my spirit would rejoice,

And leap within me at the cry)

The battle-cry of Victory!

The rain came down upon my head

Unshelter'd — and the heavy wind

Rendered me mad and deaf and blind.

It was but man, I thought, who shed

Laurels upon me: and the rush —

The torrent of the chilly air

Gurgled within my ear the crush

Of empires — with the captive's prayer —

The hum of suitors — and the tone

Of flattery 'round a sovereign's throne.

My passions, from that hapless hour,

Usurp'd a tyranny which men

Have deem'd, since I have reach'd to power;

My innate nature — be it so:

But, father, there liv'd one who, then,

Then — in my boyhood — when their fire

Burn'd with a still intenser glow,

(For passion must, with youth, expire)

E'en then who knew this iron heart

In woman's weakness had a part.

I have no words — alas! — to tell

The loveliness of loving well!

Nor would I now attempt to trace

The more than beauty of a face

Whose lineaments, upon my mind,

Are — shadows on th' unstable wind:

Thus I remember having dwelt

Some page of early lore upon,

With loitering eye, till I have felt

The letters — with their meaning — melt

To fantasies — with none.

Oh, she was worthy of all love!

Love — as in infancy was mine —

Twas such as angel minds above

Might envy; her young heart the shrine

On which my ev'ry hope and thought

Were incense — then a goodly gift,

For they were childish — and upright —

Pure —- as her young example taught:

Why did I leave it, and, adrift,

Trust to the fire within, for light?

We grew in age — and love — together,

Roaming the forest, and the wild;

My breast her shield in wintry weather —

And, when the friendly sunshine smil'd,

And she would mark the opening skies,

I saw no Heaven — but in her eyes.

Young Love's first lesson is — the heart:

For 'mid that sunshine, and those smiles,

When, from our little cares apart,

And laughing at her girlish wiles,

I'd throw me on her throbbing breast,

And pour my spirit out in tears —

There was no need to speak the rest —

No need to quiet any fears

Of her — who ask'd no reason why,

But turn'd on me her quiet eye!

Yet more than worthy of the love

My spirit struggled with, and strove,

When, on the mountain peak, alone,

Ambition lent it a new tone —

I had no being — but in thee:

The world, and all it did contain

In the earth — the air — the sea —

Its joy — its little lot of pain

That was new pleasure — the ideal,

Dim, vanities of dreams by night —

And dimmer nothings which were real —

(Shadows — and a more shadowy light!)

Parted upon their misty wings,

And, so, confusedly, became

Thine image, and — a name — a name!

Two separate — yet most intimate things.

I was ambitious — have you known

The passion, father? You have not:

A cottager, I mark'd a throne

Of half the world as all my own,

And murmur'd at such lowly lot —

But, just like any other dream,

Upon the vapor of the dew

My own had past, did not the beam

Of beauty which did while it thro'

The minute — the hour — the day — oppress

My mind with double loveliness.

We walk'd together on the crown

Of a high mountain which look'd down

Afar from its proud natural towers

Of rock and forest, on the hills —

The dwindled hills! begirt with bowers

And shouting with a thousand rills.

I spoke to her of power and pride,

But mystically — in such guise

That she might deem it nought beside

The moment's converse; in her eyes

I read, perhaps too carelessly,

A mingled feeling with my own;

The flush on her bright cheek to me

Seem'd to become a queenly throne

Too well that I should let it be

Light in the wilderness alone.

I wrapp'd myself in grandeur then,

And donn'd a visionary crown —-

Yet it was not that Fantasy

Had thrown her mantle over me,

But that, among the rabble — men —

Lion ambition is chain'd down,

And crouches to a keeper's hand;

Not so in deserts where the grand —

The wild — the terrible conspire

With their own breath to fan his fire.

Look 'round thee now on Samarcand!

Is not she queen of Earth? her pride

Above all cities? in her hand

Their destinies? in all beside

Of glory which the world hath known

Stands she not nobly and alone?

Falling — her veriest stepping-stone

Shall form the pedestal of a throne —

And who her sovereign? Timour — he

Whom the astonished people saw

Striding o'er empires haughtily

A diadem'd outlaw!

Oh! human love! thou spirit given,

On Earth, of all we hope in Heaven!

Which fall'st into the soul like rain

Upon the Sirocwither'd plain,

And failing in thy power to bless

But leav'st the heart a wilderness!

Idea! which bindest life around

With music of so strange a sound

And beauty of so wild a birth, —

Farewell! for I have won the Earth!

When Hope, the eagle that tower'd, could see

No cliff beyond him in the sky,

His pinions were bent droopingly,

And homeward turn'd his soften'd eye.

'Twas sunset: when the sun will part

There comes a sullenness of heart

To him who still would look upon

The glory of the summer sun.

That soul will hate the ev'ning mist,

So often lovely, and will list

To the sound of the coming darkness (known

To those whose spirits hearken) as one

Who, in a dream of night, would fly

But cannot from a danger nigh.

What tho' the moon — the white moon

Shed all the splendour of her noon,

Her smile is chilly — and her beam,

In that time of dreariness, will seem

(So like you gather in your breath)

A portrait taken after death.

And boyhood is a summer sun

Whose waning is the dreariest one —-

For all we live to know is known,

And all we seek to keep hath flown —

Let life, then, as the day-flower, fall

With the noon-day beauty — which is all.

I reach'd my home — my home no more —

For all had flown who made it so —

I pass'd from out its mossy door,

And, tho' my tread was soft and low,

A voice came from the threshold stone

Of one whom I had earlier known —

Oh! I defy thee, Hell, to show

On beds of fire that burn below,

A humbler heart — a deeper woe.

Father, I firmly do believe —

I know — for Death, who comes for me

From regions of the blest afar,

Where there is nothing to deceive,

Hath left his iron gate ajar,

And rays of truth you cannot see

Are flashing thro' Eternity —-

I do believe that Eblis hath

A snare in ev'ry human path —

Else how, when in the holy grove

I wandered of the idol, Love,

Who daily scents his snowy wings

With incense of burnt offerings

From the most unpolluted things,

Whose pleasant bowers are yet so riven

Above with trellis'd rays from Heaven,

No mote may shun — no tiniest fly —

The light'ning of his eagle eye —

How was it that Ambition crept,

Unseen, amid the revels there,

Till growing bold, he laughed and leapt

In the tangles of Love's very hair?

帖木儿 [1]

神父啊，弥留时仁慈的慰藉！

已不是，我（此刻）的主题——

我不再疯狂地以为人间的权力

可以赦免我那执迷不悟的、

怪诞的傲慢带来的罪愆——

我已没有沉溺或梦想的时间：

你称它希望——这火中之火！

可它只是欲望的剧痛发作：

假如我能希望——哦上帝！我能——

它的源泉就更圣洁——更神圣——

我就不会叫你傻瓜，老人，

可这希望并非你给我的礼品。

你明白一个灵魂的秘密

狂野的自豪向耻辱屈膝。

哦！渴望的心！我曾用威名

继承了你枯萎的部分，

辉煌的荣光曾照耀

我御座上镶满的珠宝，

*地狱*的光环！满怀痛苦

*地狱*也再不能使我恐怖——

哦！渴求的心，为失去的鲜花

和明媚的夏日阳光！

那死亡岁月中不死的声音，

伴随着不停歇的钟声，

用蛊惑的精灵，在你的

空虚上——敲响了丧钟。

我并非总像现在这样：

发烧的王冠戴在头上

我曾追求并篡夺权力——

恺撒曾凶猛地继承罗马——

我难道不也同他一样？

一份君王思想的遗产，

和自豪的成功奋斗精神

与全人类一起留传。

我的生命源自山村：

塔格雷的雾已把夜露

洒上我的头颅，

我相信高翔远举的竞争

和莽撞空气中的骚乱

已蛰伏在我的头发中间。

（在一个邪恶的夜梦里）

那夜露很晚才从*天庭*洒落

我头上，带着*地狱*的气息，

头上的云中红光闪烁

犹如彩旗，高高飘摇，

君主王国的壮丽景观

闪现在我半闭的眼前，

深沉的号声闷雷般咆哮

匆匆掠过我耳边，宣讲

人世的争战，我的声音，

我傻傻的声音不断膨胀！

（哦！我的心儿何等欢欣，

战斗的呐喊在心中跳荡）

胜利的呼声跳出胸膛！

大雨洒落在我的头上

毫无遮挡——大风吹得我

心乱神狂，又聋又盲。

我想，只有人才能给我

把桂冠戴上：潮水般奔涌——

寒冷的气流——帝国碾压的

轰鸣在我耳中汩汩流动——

战俘的祈祷——求婚者的絮叨——

谄媚者阿谀奉承的腔调

在君王宝座周遭萦绕。

从那倒霉时刻起，我野心勃勃，

篡夺了统治宝座，人们认为

那是暴政，因为我已大权在握；

我固有的本性吧——即便那样：

可神父啊，那时生活的那人，

正是我年轻时的模样——烈火

燃烧，放出更强烈的光芒，

（激情必然，随青春消失）

即便那时他也明白这钢铁心房

依然有一份弱女子的柔肠。

我实在——天哪！——无言倾诉

那爱中蕴含的爱意！

此刻我也不试图追寻

比那美丽容颜更多的含义，

在我心中，她的容貌体形，

只是——乱风中摇曳的身影：

于是我记起曾流连

注目早先传说的书里，

眼神散漫，直到我发现

那些书信——连带它们的意义——

熔入幻想，没有别的。

哦，她配得上人间所有的爱！

那爱——像孩提时代属于我——

那是天使也会嫉妒的爱；

她年轻的心是圣洁的场所

我的每一个希望和思想

都是那里的香——美的礼物，

它们稚嫩——正直——纯洁——

正如她展示的青春榜样：

可我为什么还要离它去漂泊，

一任内心的烈火去追逐荣光？

我们在岁月与爱情中成长，

在荒野的森林中一起徜徉；

我的胸膛是她寒冬的后盾，

而当友爱的阳光露出笑容，

她总能展示一片开阔的天空，

我看见天堂——可只在她眼中。

年轻恋人的第一课——交心：
沐浴着阳光和笑的天真，
当我们那些小小的烦恼离去，
开始嘲笑她那少女的恶作剧，
我扑上去压住她悸动的心房，
付出全部精力，热泪盈眶——
剩下的任何言说都已多余——
更无须平息她的任何恐惧——
她不再向我追问为什么这样，
安详的眼神只盯着我的脸庞！

然而除了为般配爱情追索，
我的心灵还要争取更多，
当我独自站在高山顶上，
野心让我的精神再度膨胀——
除了你那里——我已没有存在：
世界，和它拥有的全部
土地——空气——大海——
它的欢乐和小小的痛楚
都是新的欣喜—理想，
暗淡，夜梦中的所有虚荣——
更暗淡的是毫无任何真相——
（全是阴影——更阴暗的光！）

都已乘迷雾的双翼离去，

却又稀里糊涂地，变成

你的形象，和一个名字！

两个分离——却最亲密的东西。

我野心勃勃——你可清楚

那贪欲，神父啊？你不清楚：

我，一介村民，竟把半个世界

划入自己统治的版图，

还抱怨命运不够眷顾——

然而，正如一切美梦，

终将如露水化作青烟

我的美梦也一去不返，

然而美的光束依然照射

无时无刻——无日无夜——

不以双倍的爱压迫我心田。

我们曾一起漫步在高山

之巅，俯瞰壮美的大自然，

远处石塔点缀，森林繁茂

群峰秀丽，连绵不断——

渐小的山峦！凉亭环绕，

还有无数小河流水潺潺。

我向她讲述权力和自豪，

神秘地——用伪装的外衣，

好让她觉得除了此刻的闲聊，

其余无关紧要；在她眼里

我发现，也许太不经意，

一种混杂的情感和我的交织；

在我心里她颊上闪动的红霞，

宛若女王的宝座般娇艳，

那般美好，我定要让它

成为荒野中的明灯一盏。

我浑身披挂，威风凛凛，

头戴梦幻的王冠——

然而并不是*梦幻*

给我披上她斗篷的威权

而是——暴民中的——人——

雄狮的野心已被锁住，

在看守人的手下蹲伏；

也不是沙漠中大群的——

可怕的——狂徒——密谋

以便煽起他的烈火。

在*撒马尔罕*瞭望你的四周吧！

难道她不是*地球*的女王？

她的豪爽难道不是天下无双？

人们的命运难道不由她执掌？

在世人熟知的一切荣耀里

难道她不是高贵无比？

即使倒下——她的踏脚石——

也会成为御座的基石——

那么谁是她的君王？帖木儿——

一个头戴王冠的非法之徒，

惊呆的人们看到他正在

帝国的土地上高视阔步！

哦！人类的爱！你孕育精神，

我们*世*人对上苍的盼望！

爱的精神注入人们的心灵，

恰如春雨洒落凋敝的平原上，

你的权势失落真乃上天赐福，

否则人心将是一片荒芜！

思想！把生命和音乐粘结，

形成如此奇妙的调协，

和美粘结成如此狂野的诞辰——

别了！因为我已赢得了*世界*！

希望，高翔的雄鹰，当他

看不见身外的峭壁巉岩，

他的双翼便无力地垂下，

掉转温柔的眼睛飞返故园。

落日来临：太阳将离去，

心中油然生出一丝忧郁，

因为他依然念念不忘

夏日骄阳的辉煌。

那个灵魂将仇恨常有的、

美丽的黄昏薄雾，也会

倾听夜色将临的声音，

（倾听的心灵熟知此声）

犹如一个夜梦中想飞的人，

却不能从迫近的危险逃生。

如果月亮——白色的月亮

洒下午夜全部的辉光，

她的微笑清冷——她的光束，

在那个沉闷的时分，会显出

一幅死后拍摄的肖像，

（恰如你此刻看到的那样。）

男童时代是夏日的骄阳

它的衰退最令人沮丧——

因为我们想知的已知晓，

我们想保留的却已飞掉——

让生命与如日中天的美丽，

一起昙花般陨落——如此而已。。

我回到家——可家已不在——

造就这一切的，一切已飞走——

我走过的门边长满青苔，

尽管我的脚步又轻又柔，

一个声音从门槛石下传出

这声音我早年就熟知——

哦！我蔑视你，*地狱*，谅你

不敢在烧烫的火床上展现，

一颗更卑微的心——更深的哀怨。

神父啊，我明白——我深信——

我的*死亡*，已经来临

从神佑的遥远之地，

那儿没有任何谎言骗人，

*死神*已将他的铁门开启，

真理的光芒你看不见

真实只在*永恒*中闪现——

我坚信*恶魔*已在人境

每条小径布下陷阱——

否则，当我在圣林中

彷徨，怎会巧遇*爱*的偶像，

*爱*用最纯洁的贡献

把进香的祭品点燃，

天天熏香他雪白的翅膀，

他欢乐的凉亭随即被扯散

那里便充满来自*天堂*的光线，

没有尘埃——没有最小的飞虫——

能避开他雄鹰般闪光的眼睛——

狂欢中，*野心*在潜行

看不见，直到他勇气倍增，

在*爱*的美发缠绕中欢庆

那曾是一幅怎样的情景？

1　此诗首发于1827年，诗人以14世纪帖木儿帝国的统治者为题，用高度想象的笔触，以第一人称口吻，讲述主人公从一个纯真善良的山村男孩变成野心勃勃，权势熏天的帝王的经历，其中既有对舍弃爱情与青春去追求权力和名望的悔悟，也不乏对自己煌煌功业的自矜。原诗403行，后经多次修改缩减为现在的223行，诗节长短不一，韵式与格律也相对比较自由，不过，诗中较多出现的主要还是四音步抑扬格以及交韵和随韵。

Once upon a midnight dreary, while I pondered, weak and weary,

Over many a quaint and curious volume of forgotten lore,

While I nodded, nearly napping, suddenly there came a tapping,

As of some one gently rapping, rapping at my chamber door.

" Tis some visitor," I muttered, "tapping at my chamber door —

Only this, and nothing more."

Ah, distinctly I remember it was in the bleak December,

And each separate dying ember wrought its ghost upon the floor.

Eagerly I wished the morrow; — vainly I had sought to borrow

From my books surcease of sorrow — sorrow for the lost Lenore —

For the rare and radiant maiden whom the angels name Lenore —

Nameless here for evermore.

And the silken sad uncertain rustling of each purple curtain

Thrilled me — filled me with fantastic terrors never felt before;

So that now, to still the beating of my heart, I stood repeating,

" 'Tis some visitor entreating entrance at my chamber door —

Some late visitor entreating entrance at my chamber door; —

This it is, and nothing more."

Presently my soul grew stronger; hesitating then no longer,

"Sir," said I, "or Madam, truly your forgiveness I implore;

But the fact is I was napping, and so gently you came rapping,

And so faintly you came tapping, tapping at my chamber door,

That I scarce was sure I heard you" — here I opened wide the door; —

Darkness there, and nothing more.

Deep into that darkness peering, long I stood there wondering, fearing,

Doubting, dreaming dreams no mortals ever dared to dream before;

But the silence was unbroken, and the stillness gave no token,

And the only word there spoken was the whispered word, "Lenore!"

This I whispered, and an echo murmured back the word, "Lenore!" —

Merely this, and nothing more.

Back into the chamber turning, all my soul within me burning,

Soon again I heard a tapping somewhat louder than before.

"Surely," said I, "surely that is something at my window lattice:

Let me see, then, what thereat is, and this mystery explore —

Let my heart be still a moment and this mystery explore; —

'Tis the wind and nothing more."

Open here I flung the shutter, when, with many a flirt and flutter,

In there stepped a stately raven of the saintly days of yore;

Not the least obeisance made he; not a minute stopped or stayed he;

But, with mien of lord or lady, perched above my chamber door —

Perched upon a bust of Pallas just above my chamber door —

Perched, and sat, and nothing more.

Then this ebony bird beguiling my sad fancy into smiling,

By the grave and stern decorum of the countenance it wore.

"Though thy crest be shorn and shaven, thou," I said, "art sure no

craven,

Ghastly grim and ancient raven wandering from the Nightly shore —

Tell me what thy lordly name is on the Night's Plutonian shore!"

Quoth the Raven, "Nevermore."

Much I marvelled this ungainly fowl to hear discourse so plainly,

Though its answer little meaning — little relevancy bore;

For we cannot help agreeing that no living human being

Ever yet was blest with seeing bird above his chamber door —

Bird or beast upon the sculptured bust above his chamber door,

With such name as "Nevermore."

But the raven, sitting lonely on the placid bust, spoke only

That one word, as if his soul in that one word he did outpour.

Nothing farther then he uttered; not a feather then he fluttered—

Till I scarcely more than muttered, "other friends have flown before —

On the morrow he will leave me, as my hopes have flown before."

Then the bird said, "Nevermore."

Startled at the stillness broken by reply so aptly spoken,

"Doubtless," said I, "what it utters is its only stock and store,

Caught from some unhappy master whom unmerciful Disaster

Followed fast and followed faster till his songs one burden bore —

Till the dirges of his Hope that melancholy burden bore

Of 'Never—nevermore'."

But the Raven still beguiling all my fancy into smiling,

Straight I wheeled a cushioned seat in front of bird, and bust and door;

Then upon the velvet sinking, I betook myself to linking

Fancy unto fancy, thinking what this ominous bird of yore—

What this grim, ungainly, ghastly, gaunt and ominous bird of yore

Meant in croaking "Nevermore."

This I sat engaged in guessing, but no syllable expressing

To the fowl whose fiery eyes now burned into my bosom's core;

This and more I sat divining, with my head at ease reclining

On the cushion's velvet lining that the lamplight gloated o'er,

But whose velvet violet lining with the lamplight gloating o'er,

She shall press, ah, nevermore!

Then methought the air grew denser, perfumed from an unseen censer

Swung by Seraphim whose footfalls tinkled on the tufted floor.

"Wretch," I cried, "thy God hath lent thee — by these angels he hath sent thee

Respite — respite and nepenthe, from thy memories of Lenore!

Quaff, oh quaff this kind nepenthe and forget this lost Lenore!"

Quoth the Raven, "Nevermore."

"Prophet!" said I, "thing of evil! — prophet still, if bird or devil! —

Whether Tempter sent, or whether tempest tossed thee here ashore,

Desolate yet all undaunted, on this desert land enchanted —

On this home by horror haunted — tell me truly, I implore —

Is there — is there balm in Gilead? — tell me — tell me, I implore!"

Quoth the Raven, "Nevermore."

"Prophet!" said I, "thing of evil- prophet still, if bird or devil!

By that Heaven that bends above us — by that God we both adore —

Tell this soul with sorrow laden if, within the distant Aidenn,

It shall clasp a sainted maiden whom the angels name Lenore —

Clasp a rare and radiant maiden whom the angels name Lenore."

Quoth the Raven, "Nevermore."

"Be that word our sign in parting, bird or fiend," I shrieked, upstarting —

"Get thee back into the tempest and the Night's Plutonian shore!

Leave no black plume as a token of that lie thy soul hath spoken!

Leave my loneliness unbroken! — quit the bust above my door!

Take thy beak from out my heart, and take thy form from off my door!"

Quoth the Raven, "Nevermore."

And the Raven, never flitting, still is sitting, still is sitting

On the pallid bust of Pallas just above my chamber door;

And *his* eyes have all the seeming of a demon's that is dreaming,

And the lamplight o'er him streaming throws his shadow on the floor;

And my soul from out that shadow that lies floating on the floor

Shall be lifted — nevermore!

乌鸦[1]

从前在一个凄凉的子夜，我冥想着，神疲力竭，

冥想许多稀奇古怪的、被人遗忘的学问，

我垂着头，正睡眼迷离，突然传来一声敲击，

仿佛有人在叩击，叩击我卧室的门。

"客来了罢，"我呢喃着，"正敲我的房门——

如此而已，别无它闻。"

哦，分明地我想起，那正是萧瑟的十二月里，

每一团余烬行将消熄，在地板上投下鬼影绰绰。

热切地，我期盼着天光；徒劳地，我一直在想望

用阅读来终止忧伤——忧伤，为了失去的莱诺[2]，

为了那光彩照人的绝代女郎，天使们称她莱诺——

可这名字在这儿已永远沉默。

那每一块紫色的丝绸窗帘，悲哀地不停抖颤，

令我恐惧——使我心中充满前所未有的异样的阴森；

所以此刻，为镇定我悸动的心，我伫立着反复沉吟

"那是一位来客在恳请，恳请进入我卧室的门，

一位夤夜的来客在恳请，恳请进入我卧室的门，

就此而已，别无它闻。”

于是我的心儿变得坚强，不再犹豫，不再彷徨，
“先生，”我说，“或夫人，我真心抱歉，求您开恩；
事实是，我刚才小睡未醒，而您来敲门又那样轻，
您来敲门是那样轻，那样轻敲我的房门，
因此，我几乎不相信我听见了您。”——于是我敞开房门——
黑暗而已，别无它闻。

深深地凝视着那片黑暗，我良久伫立，心疑而胆寒，
疑惑中梦见任何凡人都不敢做的梦；
可岑寂依旧延长，黑暗也没有改变迹象，
只有一个字响在口上，那低诉着的字，“莱诺！”
我低诉着，一个回声把那字悄然送还，“莱诺！”
仅此而已，余皆索寞。

我返身再回房中，我的灵魂整个儿在灼痛，
很快我又听到那响动，一声比刚才略大的剥啄。
“肯定，”我说，“肯定有什么在弄我的窗棂；
那么让我看看，什么在窗棂，再将那秘密探索——
让我的心儿安静片刻，再将那秘密探索——
风声而已，别无什么！”

猛然我把窗户推开，出现阵阵翅膀的击拍，

一只庄重的乌鸦飞进屋来，带着昔日圣洁的容光；

它丝毫不向我致敬点头；也没有一刻的停留，

却以贵人命妇的派头，栖息在我的房门上——

栖息在我门上的一尊半身帕拉斯[3]雕像上——

端坐在那里，别无它样。

于是，这只黑鸟将我忧伤的幻觉逗弄成微笑，

以它满脸的矜持和做作的庄严，

"尽管你修剪过冠毛，"我说，"你绝非一只怯鸟，

也非幽灵般的古鸟，漂泊自*夜*的海边，

告诉我你高贵的名字，在*夜之冥冥*的彼岸！"

可那乌鸦说，"永不再现。"

我惊讶不已，这不雅的怪鸟，竟能听得如此明了，

虽然它的回答没有意义，也没有任何关联；

可我们不能不同意，世间还无人有这样的运气，

居然能够看见飞鸟栖息在自己的房门上边——

看见飞鸟或禽兽栖息在他门上的半身雕像上面，

还有这样的名字"永不再现"。

然而那乌鸦，孤独地坐了，在平静的像上，仅仅说了

那一个字眼，仿佛它把自己的灵魂铸进了那个字眼。

于是它不再出一声，也不抖动羽毛一根，

直到我耳语几乎无声，"别的朋友们早已星散，

明晨它也要离我而去，正如我从前的希望已飞散。"

那乌鸦才说，"永不再现。"

沉寂被打断竟是如此巧妙的答案令我讶然，

"无疑，"我说，"它说的是它唯一的语言，

从某位不幸的先生学来，而他曾被一连串无情的灾难

紧紧追赶，愈追愈快，直到他的歌载着沉重的悲叹，

他的希望的挽歌中出现了这一忧伤的字眼：

永不——永不再现。"

但那大鸟依旧把我所有的幻觉逗弄成微笑，

我立即推一轮椅垫，到门边像下和鸟的面前；

然后坐在天鹅绒垫上，开始陷入无边的联想，

奇思连着异想，思量这不祥的古鸟何出此言，

这狰狞、丑陋、精灵、古怪、不祥的古鸟何出此言，

何以要呱呱叫着"永不再现"。

就这样我静坐猜度，但对那鸟一个音节也未发出，

它那火热的双眼，此刻直烧入我的心坎；

我猜想这字眼和更多的意思，头儿自然地斜倚，

悠闲地斜倚，在洒满灯光的天鹅绒衬垫，

可那悠闲地斜倚着洒满灯光的天鹅绒紫垫，

她再也不能倚靠，哦，永不再现！

于是我想着，空气密度增长，被看不见的香炉熏香，

天使们挥舞着香炉，丁零的脚步声响在铺草的地面。

"可怜虫，"我喊道，"上帝派天使来给你送药，

这药能把你的心病治疗，中止你对莱诺的思念！

哦，让我痛饮这忘忧药吧，忘却对失去的莱诺的思念！"

乌鸦说，"永不再现。"

"先知！"我说，"不祥的东西——仍是先知，无论是鸟是魑！

无论是魔鬼派你，还是暴风雨抛你，到这里的岸边，

凄凉孤寂，却毫不泄气，在这荒芜而受到妖惑的土地——

在这被恐怖作祟的屋里——请真实地告诉我，求你见怜，

有吗，有基列香膏吗[4]——告诉我，告诉我，求你见怜！"

乌鸦说，"永不再现。"

"先知！"我说，"不祥的东西——仍是先知，无论是鸟是魑！

凭着我们头顶的天堂，凭着我们都崇拜的*主上*，

告诉我这充满哀伤的灵魂，在那遥远的*爱顿*，[5]

他能否拥抱那圣洁的灵魂，被天使称作莱诺的女郎，

能否拥抱那光彩流溢的佳人，被天使称作莱诺的女郎。"

乌鸦说，"永无想望。"

"让此言作我们分别的留念，鸟或魔！"我站起尖声呼喊，

"回到你的暴风雨中去，回到你那*暗夜的冥海之滨*！

别留下黑羽作标记，以免我把你撒谎的灵魂想起！

别打破我完整的孤寂！离开我的雕像和房门！

撤回你的嘴，从我心上，撤回你的形，从我的房门！"

可乌鸦说，"永不可能。"

而那乌鸦，毫无动静，居然端坐不动，端坐不动，

高踞于苍白的帕拉斯像顶，正好俯视我的房门；

它的目光简直就像，一位做梦的魔王，

洒在它身上的灯光在地上投射出它的阴影，

而从它漂移在地上的阴影中，我的灵魂将会飞升

将会飞升——永不可能！

1　这首诗首发于1845年1月29日的《纽约晚镜报》，讲述一只硕大的乌鸦在一个凄凉的冬夜，突然飞落在一位学者房门上，不断复述着一个词"nevermore"的故事。这位学者刚刚失去了爱人Lenore，正处在巨大的悲痛之中，乌鸦的突然造访并向他不断重复的这个词，不仅营造了一种神秘的氛围，更加重了他的哀伤。全诗18节，每节6行，共108行。此作采用了复杂的结构与韵律。其基本格律是八音步扬抑格，但也间杂有不完全的四音步和七音步。在用韵方面，除脚韵外，也大量使用内韵和头韵。就脚韵而言，采用ABCBBB 的韵式，如果算上内韵则成为：AA B CC CB B B的韵式，也即第 1 和3 两句大都有内韵，第4句句中与第3句脚韵相押，因此读来极富音乐性。

2　Lenore 是坡诗中数次出现的一位早逝的美女，象征诗人的妻子、恋人、生母和养母等人。一般译作"莱诺儿"，这里出于押韵的需要，权且译作"莱诺"。

3　Pallas, 希腊神话中的众多神名，一般指雅典娜等女神，也指泰坦巨人等男神。

4　《圣经》中说，基列所产的香膏具有医治多种病的作用。故在后来的文学作品中常被引申为可治疗百病的灵丹妙药。

5　Aidenn源自希伯来语，即圣经中的伊甸园（Eden），常出现在文学作品中。

BRIDAL BALLAD

The ring is on my hand,

And the wreath is on my brow;

Satins and jewels grand

Are all at my command,

And I am happy now.

And my lord he loves me well;

But when first he breathed his vow

I felt my bosom swell—

For the words rang as a knell,

And the voice seemed his who fell

In the battle down the dell,

And who is happy now.

But he spoke to reassure me,

And he kissed my pallid brow,

While a reverie came o'er me,

And to the churchyard bore me,

And I sighed to him before me,

Thinking him dead D'Elormie,

"Oh, I am happy now!"

And thus the words were spoken,

And this the plighted vow,

And though my faith be broken,

And though my heart be broken,

Behold the golden token

That *proves* me happy now!

Would God I could awaken!

For I dream I know not how,

And my soul is sorely shaken

Lest an evil step be taken,—

Lest the dead who is forsaken

May not be happy now.

新娘谣 ¹

戒指戴在手上，
花冠戴在头上；
锦缎和珠宝成堆
全都归我执掌，
我现在很幸福。

夫君爱我发狂；
可当他发誓爱我
我却感到胸腔憋涨——
他的话如丧钟敲响，
那声音好像说*他*已倒下
倒在深山幽谷的战场，
而他现在很幸福。

他温柔地安慰我，
轻吻我苍白的前额，
乘我迷乱之时，
把我拥进教堂，

我对着面前的*他*叹息，

觉得他是已死的德洛尔密，

"哦，我现在很幸福！"

这话脱口而出，

便成了宣誓的婚约，

虽然我的信誓已毁，

我的心儿已破碎，

看着这金色的信物，

它*证明*我此刻很幸福！

愿上帝让我清醒！

睡梦里我无法看清，

我的灵魂在痛苦地颤抖

担心他采取邪恶的步骤——

担心死者被彻底弃绝

他现在可能不幸福。

1　此诗首发于1837年，原题《谣曲》。1841年重发时改作《新娘谣》。据说坡这诗的灵感来
　　自一份小杂志上刊登的一首古老的苏格兰民谣，写一个夫人被迫与心爱的人分手，改适他
　　人的故事，坡这里写一个姑娘得知爱人战死疆场而昏厥，醒来却发现自己在一个朋友的怀
　　抱中，在心神恍惚中，她误以为拥抱着自己的正是自己的爱人德洛尔密而接受了他，而爱
　　着他的这位朋友却以为她同意和他结婚。这诗模仿苏格兰谣曲的形式，以新娘自己口吻，
　　写出了她新婚的情景与发现真相后的痛苦与悔恨。

In Heaven a spirit doth dwell

"Whose heart-strings are a lute";

None sing so wildly well

As the angel Israfel,

And the giddy stars (so legends tell),

Ceasing their hymns, attend the spell

Of his voice, all mute.

Tottering above

In her highest noon,

The enamored moon

Blushes with love,

While, to listen, the red levin

(With the rapid Pleiads, even,

Which were seven)

Pauses in Heaven.

And they say (the starry choir

And the other listening things)

That Israfeli's fire

Is owing to that lyre

By which he sits and sings —

The trembling living wire

Of those unusual strings.

But the skies that angel trod,

Where deep thoughts are a duty —

Where Love's a grown-up God —

Where the Houri glances are

Imbued with all the beauty

Which we worship in a star.

Therefore thou art not wrong,

Israfeli, who despises

An unimpassioned song;

To thee the laurels belong,

Best bard, because the wisest!

Merrily live, and long!

The ecstasies above

With thy burning measures suit —

Thy grief, thy joy, thy hate, thy love,

With the fervor of thy lute-

Well may the stars be mute!

Yes, Heaven is thine; but this

Is a world of sweets and sours;

Our flowers are merely — flowers,

And the shadow of thy perfect bliss

Is the sunshine of ours.

If I could dwell

Where Israfel

Hath dwelt, and he where I

He might not sing so widely well

A mortal melody,

While a bolder note than this might swell

From my lyre within the sky.

以斯拉斐尔[1]

天堂住着一位神灵
"他的心弦是一把诗琴";
没人能像天使以斯拉斐尔
唱得那般曼妙,那般清纯,
(传说)那些招摇的星辰
全都停止歌唱,被这声音
迷倒,统统失声。

月亮在午夜的中天
摇摇欲坠地蹒跚,
对这歌声满心爱慕
娇羞得烧红了脸,
红色的闪电停下脚步
(甚至天上的昴宿星团,
迅捷的七颗明星)
也停下来一同静听。

他们(唱诗班的星辰

和其余静听的物体）说
以斯拉斐尔的火热激情
正是来自那把七弦琴
他倚琴而坐，抚琴歌吟——
震颤的琴声包孕生命
非凡的琴弦奏出天音。

在天使涉足的天庭，
深沉的思想是一种责任——
那里爱情是成熟的神——
那里霍丽女神[2]的秋波里，
浸透着我们崇拜星辰
所具有的全部美丽。

因此，以斯拉斐尔，
你蔑视毫无激情的歌唱
没有丝毫不妥当；
桂冠属于你这最佳歌手，
因为你有最智慧的歌唱！
愿你生活得快乐，久长！

上天的销魂状态
和着你燃烧的旋律——

你的哀、乐、恨、爱，

和你的琴弦一起鼓荡，

让星辰不再发出声响！

不错，天堂是你的；可这

世界充满酸甜苦辣；

我们的花不过是——花，

而你极乐至福的身影

却把我们置于阳光下。

倘若我能够

和以斯拉斐尔

互换居住的地方

他未必能将人间曲调

唱得那般美妙，

而也许我的竖琴在天上

也能涌出更大胆的吟唱。

1   此作写于西点军校时期，1831年首发，1836年修改。据坡自己说，以斯拉斐尔是可兰经中
     的天使，他的心是一把诗琴，能唱出天上最美妙的歌。坡颇有以以斯拉斐尔自许的意思。
     有论者将这首颇具东方色彩的诗歌与柯勒律治的《忽必烈汗》相提并论。此作8节，诗律
     不一。
2   伊斯兰教天堂中的美女。

EULALIE—A SONG

I dwelt alone

In a world of moan,

And my soul was a stagnant tide,

Till the fair and gentle Eulalie became my blushing bride —

Till the yellow-haired young Eulalie became my smiling bride.

Ah, less — less bright

The stars of the night

Than the eyes of the radiant girl!

And never a flake

That the vapor can make

With the moon-tints of purple and pearl,

Can vie with the modest Eulalie's most unregarded curl —

Can compare with the bright-eyed Eulalie's most humble and careless curl.

Now Doubt — now Pain

Come never again,

For her soul gives me sigh for sigh,

And all day long

Shines, bright and strong,

Astarté within the sky,

While ever to her dear Eulalie upturns her matron eye —

While ever to her young Eulalie upturns her violet eye.

尤乐丽——歌 ¹

我独居一方

在哀吟的世上,

我的灵魂是死水一潭,

直到美丽温柔的尤乐丽成为我羞涩的新娘——

直到年轻金发的尤乐丽成为我微笑的新娘。

哦,夜晚的星光

远远——远远比不上

那容光焕发的少女双眼明亮!

没有一片一缕

水汽凝聚而成的

月色染成的紫露和珍珠,

能与谦虚的尤乐丽最不惹人注目的卷发匹配——

能与眼睛漂亮的尤乐丽最谦卑最自然的卷发媲美。

往昔的*怀疑*——*悲痛*

再也不见踪影,

她的灵魂和我的息息相通,

天上的爱神哟

明亮又强壮，

整日放射光芒，

亲爱的尤乐丽抬起少妇的眼神转向她——

年轻的尤乐丽抬起紫色的眼睛转向她。

1   此作首发于1845年的《美国评论》。有论者认为，此作表现了诗人婚后的情形。诗句长短
     不一，诗律不一。有艺术家将其谱写成歌曲吟唱。

THE CONQUEROR WORM

Lo! 'tis a gala night

Within the lonesome latter years!

An angel throng, bewinged, bedight

In veils, and drowned in tears,

Sit in a theatre, to see

A play of hopes and fears,

While the orchestra breathes fitfully

The music of the spheres.

Mimes, in the form of God on high,

Mutter and mumble low,

And hither and thither fly —

Mere puppets they, who come and go

At bidding of vast formless things

That shift the scenery to and fro,

Flapping from out their Condor wings

Invisible Woe!

That motley drama — oh, be sure

It shall not be forgot!

With its Phantom chased for evermore,

By a crowd that seize it not,

Through a circle that ever returneth in

To the self-same spot,

And much of Madness, and more of Sin,

And Horror the soul of the plot.

But see, amid the mimic rout

A crawling shape intrude!

A blood-red thing that writhes from out

The scenic solitude!

It writhes! — it writhes! — with mortal pangs

The mimes become its food,

And seraphs sob at vermin fangs

In human gore imbued.

Out — out are the lights — out all!

And, over each quivering form,

The curtain, a funeral pall,

Comes down with the rush of a storm,

While the angels, all pallid and wan,

Uprising, unveiling, affirm

That the play is the tragedy, "Man,"

And its hero the Conqueror Worm.

征服者害虫 [1]

看哪！这是狂欢的夜晚

在那孤独的残年里！

天使们坐在剧场观看

一场希望和恐惧的戏，

她们身披羽翼，薄纱包头，

装束俏丽，泪流不止，

乐队把星辰的音乐演奏，

忽紧忽慢，有如抽搐的呼吸。

丑角们扮成天神亮相，

哝哝唧唧，叽叽咕咕，

不过是一群傀儡的形象，

他们这里那里飞来飞去，

听命于巨大无形的外物，

这外物令场景瞬息万变，

从*猛禽*的翅膀拍出

看不见的悲哀与苦难！

哦，这杂乱无章的丑剧，

绝不能被忘记！

丑角们总在追它的*幻象*

却总无法把它抓在手里，

他们总是返回原点，

如同圆周运动的轨迹，

太多的*疯狂、罪恶和恐惧*

便是这剧情的要义。

看哪，在扮演的溃败中

一个爬行的形体侵入！

那血红的东西蠕动，

从孤独的场景爬出！

它蠕动！——忍着致命的剧痛

丑角们变成了它的食物，

天使们面对害虫大恸

它的毒牙刺进人的肌肤。

熄灭了——熄灭了所有的灯！

大幕随风暴一起落下，

罩住了每一个颤抖的身形

有如丧葬仪式的棺架，

天使们脸色苍白，充满恐惧，

全体起立，摘去面纱宣称

这是一场名为"人"的悲剧，

它的主角是*征服者害虫*。

---

1 此作首发于1843年，后来引入短篇小说《莱吉亚》中。写如戏的人生在疯狂、罪恶与恐惧等无名外力控制下，难逃悲剧的命运，最终必被死神征服。全诗5节40行，每节均用ABABCBCB韵式。

The bowers whereat, in dreams, I see

The wantonest singing birds,

Are lips — and all thy melody

Of lip-begotten words —

Thine eyes, in Heaven of heart enshrined

Then desolately fall,

O God! on my funereal mind

Like starlight on a pall —

Thy heart — thy heart! — I wake and sigh,

And sleep to dream till day

Of truth that gold can never buy —

Of the baubles that it may.

致——[1]

梦中我看见闺阁凉亭，

最放肆的鸟儿在那儿歌唱，

你的歌声虽优美动听，

可毫无诚意，全在唇上。

你的眼睛曾藏在心的天堂

而今却凄凉地落下，

哦，上帝，落在我悲哀的心上

犹如星光笼罩着棺架。

你的心——你的心！我醒来叹息，

又进入梦境，直到有一天

真情不再被金钱买断，

不再被廉价的情感欺骗。

---

1   此作收于1829年的诗集中，写失去爱的悲凉与绝望。

Beloved! amid the earnest woes

That crowd around my earthly path —

(Drear path, alas! where grows

Not even one lonely rose) —

My soul at least a solace hath

In dreams of thee, and therein knows

An Eden of bland repose.

And thus thy memory is to me

Like some enchanted far-off isle

In some tumultuous sea —

Some ocean throbbing far and free

With storms — but where meanwhile

Serenest skies continually

Just o'er that one bright island smile.

致F——[1]

爱人啊！深沉的悲伤
充斥着我的人生之路——
（哦！那阴郁的路满目荒凉
甚至没一枝孤独的玫瑰生长）——
我的灵魂至少获得一丝安抚
因为我梦见了你，因此踏上
可以安息的伊甸天堂。

于是我脑海中你的记忆
犹如远方迷人的小岛
在那汹涌的大海里——
在自由遥远的大洋里荡漾
那里不时袭来风暴，
但同时最清澈的天空持续
面对那明媚的小岛微笑。

Thou wouldst be loved? — then let thy heart

From its present pathway part not!

Being everything which now thou art,

Be nothing which thou art not.

So with the world thy gentle ways,

Thy grace, thy more than beauty,

Shall be an endless theme of praise,

And love — a simple duty.

致F——s S.O——d [1]

你想被爱吗？ ——那就让你的心

不要偏离现在的正道！

让你的一切保持本真，

绝不与本真的你分道扬镳。

用你温柔的方式与世相与，

你的优雅、超美的品格，

必将受到无尽的赞许，

爱——只是简明的职责。[2]

1　此诗最初题作《致伊丽莎白》，发表于1835年，诗中的"你"指坡曾任编辑的一份文学杂
　　志老板的女儿伊丽莎白·怀特。后几经修改，最终以现标题发表于1845年。诗题中的F—s
　　S.o——d 即女诗人弗朗西斯·萨金特·奥斯古德。
2　坡早期的诗作大都篇幅短小，形式与意象比较单纯，色调明朗，情绪也相对高昂，此作即
　　其一。这类作品似乎可作较为灵活且富有创意的"翻译"，不过，如何使其不致在形式与
　　内容两方面过分远离原诗却是极难把握的。现不揣谫陋，姑仿坊间流传的某些较好的样
　　例，以七言的形式作一尝试，或可聊备一格：
　　卿欲人爱先爱人，
　　反躬自问视己心。
　　克己惟求守正道，
　　遇事不可离本真。
　　容颜秀美且艳艳，
　　风姿典雅更彬彬。
　　若能守此与世俱，
　　何愁亲爱不近身。

Helen, thy beauty is to me

Like those Nicean barks of yore,

That gently, o'er a perfumed sea,

The weary, wayworn wanderer bore

To his own native shore.

On desperate seas long wont to roam,

Thy hyacinth hair, thy classic face,

Thy Naiad airs have brought me home

To the glory that was Greece

And the grandeur that was Rome.

Lo! in yon brilliant window-niche

How statue-like I see thee stand!

The agate lamp within thy hand.

Ah, Psyche, from the regions which

Are Holy Land!

致海伦¹

海伦，你的美在我心里

犹如尼西亚昔日的三桅船，

优雅地在芳香的海上往返，

将疲乏，困顿的游子

送回他故乡的海岸。

惯于在险恶的大海飘荡，

你风信子的发，古典的脸庞，

你仙女般的神采带我回家乡

回到古代希腊的荣耀

回到古代罗马的辉煌。

看哪！在那亮丽的窗龛里

我看见你雕像般伫立！

玛瑙灯高擎在你手中。

塞姬²女神啊，你来自

那片神圣的土地！

1　坡诗中有两首《致海伦》，这里选收的发表于1831年，1845年曾做过小修改。现在一般看到的都是1845年修订版。诗中的海伦指他儿时一位同学的母亲简·斯坦纳德。这个女人是坡幼年崇敬、热爱的对象，在坡的心目中，她不仅是一个惹人爱怜的美丽女性，也是一个仁慈、伟大的母亲。

2　希腊罗马神话中爱神的恋人；希腊语意为"心灵"。

TO THE RIVER

Fair river! in thy bright, clear flow

Of crystal, wandering water,

Thou art an emblem of the glow

Of beauty — the unhidden heart —

The playful maziness of art

In old Alberto's daughter;

But when within thy wave she looks —

Which glistens then, and trembles —

Why, then, the prettiest of brooks

Her worshipper resembles;

For in his heart, as in thy stream,

Her image deeply lies —

His heart which trembles at the beam

Of her soul-searching eyes.

致河 [1]

美丽的河！明亮，清澈，

水晶般的，蜿蜒，曲折，

你是闪光的美的标志，

——你敞开的心在清流里——

有如欢乐的艺术迷宫

在老阿尔贝托女儿心里；

她的形象在你的波浪里——

闪闪发光，颤动不止——

哦，崇拜她的人儿

正像那最美的小溪；

她的形象深藏他心里

如同在你的河流里，

她的眼光能看穿灵魂

让他的心儿颤抖不已。

---

1   写于1828年，收在《艾尔·阿拉夫、帖木儿及其他》诗集中。作品写对爱情、美的追求。

193

TO ONE IN PARADISE

Thou wast all that to me, love,

For which my soul did pine —

A green isle in the sea, love,

A fountain and a shrine,

All wreathed with fairy fruits and flowers,

And all the flowers were mine.

Ah, dream too bright to last!

Ah, starry Hope! that didst arise

But to be overcast!

A voice from out the Future cries,

"On! on!" — but o'er the Past

(Dim gulf!) my spirit hovering lies

Mute, motionless, aghast!

For, alas! alas! with me

The light of Life is o'er!

"No more — no more — no more —"

(Such language holds the solemn sea

To the sands upon the shore)

Shall bloom the thunder-blasted tree,

Or the stricken eagle soar!

And all my days are trances,

And all my nightly dreams

Are where thy dark eye glances,

And where thy footstep gleams —

In what ethereal dances,

By what eternal streams.

致天堂中的人 [1]

你是我的一切，亲爱的，

我的灵魂为你憔悴，

你是海中一片绿岛，亲爱的，

一股清泉，一片圣地，

鲜花和美果将你环绕，

所有的鲜花都曾是我的。

啊，梦太美好，难于久长！

啊，灿若星辰的希望！升起

却很快被乌云遮挡！

一个来自*未来*的声音呼喊，

"前进!"——可已超越过去，

我的心灵徘徊在（昏暗的海湾）

惊悚，呆立，无声无息！

天哪！天哪！对我而言

生命之光已经熄灭！

"不再——不再——不再"

（这话儿攫住了肃穆的大海

让她在大海的沙岸上凝滞）

让雷电击损的树木开花，

让受伤的苍鹰翱翔天际！

我所有的日子进入昏睡，

我所有的夜晚变成梦境

你的黑眼睛在那里掠过，

你的脚步在那里闪烁——

在轻歌曼舞的天上，

在永远流淌的溪流旁。

1　　此诗写作于1833年，最初出现在一个短篇作品中，没有题目，后几经改动，于1843年发表
　　在《星期六博物馆》杂志上。作品表达了对爱情、理想和一切美好事物的憧憬以及屡遭挫
　　折与失败后痛苦与绝望的心境。

TO MY MOTHER

Because I feel that, in the Heavens above,

The angels, whispering to one another,

Can find, among their burning terms of love,

None so devotional as that of "Mother,"

Therefore by that dear name I long have called you—

You who are more than mother unto me,

And fill my heart of hearts, where Death installed you

In setting my Virginia's spirit free.

My mother—my own mother, who died early,

Was but the mother of myself; but you

Are mother to the one I loved so dearly,

And thus are dearer than the mother I knew

By that infinity with which my wife

Was dearer to my soul than its soul-life.

致我的母亲[1]

我想高高在上的天堂里，

天使们，正窃窃私语，

她们发现炽烈的爱的言词里，

"母亲"是最能奉献的用语。

因此我长期以母亲称你——

对我而言你比母亲更亲，

在解放弗吉尼娅的灵魂时，

*死神*便把你深藏在我内心。

我的母亲——我那早年去世的母亲

她只是我自己的母亲，可你

却养育了我深爱的爱人，

因此比我的母亲更亲密，

我爱人的爱无边无际

对我的灵魂比生命更亲密。

1 此作首发于1849年7月，是诗人最后的诗篇之一。诗中的"母亲"指他的岳母，坡与她的关系比他幼年去世的母亲更亲密。此作用莎士比亚十四行诗的韵式。

图书在版编目（CIP）数据

多雷插图本《乌鸦——爱伦·坡诗选》/ (美) 埃德
加·爱伦·坡著；刘象愚，董滨译. —长春：吉林出
版集团股份有限公司，2015.8
ISBN 978-7-5581-6074-5

Ⅰ.①多… Ⅱ.①埃… ②刘… ③董… Ⅲ.①诗集—
美国—现代 Ⅳ.①I712.25

中国版本图书馆CIP数据核字（2018）第266928号

多雷插图本《乌鸦——爱伦·坡诗选》

著　　者	［美］埃德加·爱伦·坡
译　　者	刘象愚　董　滨
选题策划	徐家康
责任编辑	齐　琳　史俊南
装帧设计	山川at山川制本workshop
开　　本	787mm×1092mm　1/16
字　　数	130千
印　　张	13
版　　次	2019年1月第1版
印　　次	2019年1月第1次印刷
出　　版	吉林出版集团股份有限公司
电　　话	总编办：010-63109269
	发行部：010-81282844
印　　刷	天津市丰富彩艺印刷有限公司

ISBN 978-7-5581-6074-5　　　　　定价：58.00元